Father Murphy's
❧ FIRST ❧
MIRACLE

Father Murphy's ·∹❡ FIRST ❡∻· MIRACLE

novelization by
ELIZABETH LEVY

RANDOM HOUSE
New York

Library of Congress Cataloging in Publication Data:

Levy, Elizabeth.
    Father Murphy's first miracle.

    Summary: A troubled young girl's affection for the goldminer who
poses as a priest to keep an orphan school open endangers the school and
threatens the orphans with the prospect of a workhouse. [1. Orphans—
Fiction.   2. School stories]   I. Title.
PZ7.L5827Fat   1983   [Fic]   82-20516
ISBN: 0-394-85810-7

Manufactured in the United States of America
1 2 3 4 5 6 7 8 9 0

CHAPTER

1

Murphy woke up with a cold, damp feeling under his arm. "Mine," he muttered, "get your snout out of there." The big golden dog didn't move. Murphy rolled over carefully so as not to disturb him. Then Mine's tail thumped on the bed and Murphy scratched him. "Another day, boy," Murphy whispered. He swung his feet over the cot and stood up. His head almost reached the rafters.

Murphy glanced over at his partner, Moses Gage, sleeping just a few feet away.

Moses opened one eye. "Good mornin', Murphy," he grunted. He rolled out of bed. Moses was a lean black man in his late forties with just a touch of gray in his hair. Even at six a.m. he had an elegant air about him.

Murphy poured some icy water from a pitcher into a bowl and splashed it onto his face. His cheeks and forehead were lined from years of working outdoors, doing odd jobs, looking for gold. But his eyes weren't hard like some prospectors' eyes.

Murphy finished washing up and sat on Moses's bed. Mine bounced from bed to bed wagging his tail. "You're sitting on my shirt," complained Moses.

"I suppose you think you're doing me a favor by pressing it, since you outweigh me by a hundred pounds."

"Moses, I always sit over here to put on my boots. Besides, if you had woken up earlier, we wouldn't be having this problem."

Murphy pulled on his boots, looking around the loft that he and Moses shared. It was built above an abandoned saloon about ten miles outside of Jackson City in the Dakota Territory. The loft was much too crowded for two grown men and a dog. Murphy felt that it was time to move on. Too many people were growing to depend on him. Mae Woodward, the schoolteacher who had turned the abandoned saloon into a school and orphanage—she depended on him. And then there were the children. Twenty children depended on John Murphy. Murphy frowned. He didn't like it. He didn't like anybody depending on him.

Mine bounced at the top of the stairs, ready to go outside. He looked back at Murphy expectantly. "One second, Mine," mumbled Murphy. Nobody knew whether Murphy called his dog Mine because Mine was found in a mine shaft or because Mine was the only thing Murphy would admit he was attached to. Murphy's father had been killed in a mining accident when Murphy was twelve. Ever since then Murphy had been a loner. That's not quite correct. Murphy liked to think of himself as a loner.

Over the past year Murphy had gotten himself in the oddest situation of his life. To most people in the area he was known as Father Murphy, the priest helping Mae Woodward take care of the children of a group of prospectors killed in what was known as "the terrible accident." But Murphy was no priest. Every morning he woke up and told himself that his charade had to end. It was time for him to move on.

This morning was no different. "Moses, we can't go on like this," said Murphy.

"I know. We're much too crowded." Moses picked up his wrinkled shirt and put it on. When he stretched out his arm to pull on the sleeve, he hit Murphy in the stomach.

"I wasn't just talking about crowded," said Murphy. "Every morning I wake up feeling guilty. I'm the last man who should go around masquerading as a priest."

Moses pushed Mine out of the way so that he could pull on his own boots. "Well, it's no good complaining about something you can't do anything about. You've got to continue to be 'Father' Murphy or those children will be sent to the workhouse. You know you can't let Howard Rodman get them."

Murphy scowled to himself. He hated the situation, just hated it. But Moses was right. Murphy could see no way out. Without a priest as a full-time resident, the territorial authorities would close Mae Woodward's orphanage. No priest was available, so Murphy pretended to be one.

If the orphanage closed, the children would be sent to Claymore, a workhouse where orphans were treated like slaves. Howard Rodman ran the workhouse, and he made a fine profit from it. His only problem was that he worked the children so hard that they often collapsed. Rodman was in constant need of fresh supplies.

If Howard Rodman ever found out that John Murphy was not a real priest, he'd force the children into his workhouse so quickly they wouldn't know what hit them. And so each day John Murphy decided again to stay and help Mae Woodward just a little longer.

Moses and Murphy finished dressing. Mine wagged his tail and bounded down the stairs, nearly knocking Moses off his feet. "If you think it's crowded now," said Moses, "wait till Father Parker gets here. Then you'll *really* see crowded."

Murphy went outside and hitched the mules to the wagon. The countryside was rocky and too dry for much farming. The Black Hills dwarfed the land, making even John Murphy feel small, but Mae Woodward and the children had forced a small miracle out of the dry land. They raised chickens and some vegetables, enough to support themselves. They were orphans, but they didn't need anyone's charity. Mae had helped the children get over the terrible loss when all their parents had been killed in one blazing inferno. She taught them much more than how to read and write. She taught them self-respect and she gave them love.

Several months had passed since the tragedy. The land was green again. Wildflowers bloomed everywhere—wild daisies, purple asters, the delicate columbine. Mae Woodward had made a home for the children, and John Murphy knew that he couldn't abandon them until he was sure they were safe from Rodman. But how? Was he going to be stuck here forever? His masquerade couldn't last. It was a ridiculous position for a man to be in, jumping into a priest's robes every time Rodman's buggy came up the road.

John Murphy sighed and decided it was much too beautiful a day to worry. He climbed into the wagon and Mine jumped up onto the seat next to him. Mae Woodward came out, shading her eyes against the bright sun. She was a woman in her early thirties, a spinster. In the 1870s everyone knew that a thirty-year-old woman who wasn't married would never marry. Yet Mae Woodward wasn't an old woman by any means. Oh, her skin was brown from hard work in the sun. There were some lines around her eyes, but her eyes were beautiful, changing from gray to blue with her moods. Her chin was firm and it jutted out more than a woman's chin should, but her fine blonde hair softened her face. All the children thought she was beautiful.

John Murphy thought she was beautiful, too, but he never told her that. John Murphy told himself he was not good with words, and because he told himself that, he gave himself an excuse never to tell anyone what he was feeling.

Mae walked out to the wagon, trailed by three or four of the children, and looked up at Murphy. "Are you leaving now to pick up Father Parker?" she asked.

"Yes. I shouldn't be gone long if the stage is on

time." Murphy smiled down at Mae. "I've got room for one more if you want to go with me."

"You know I have to teach school," said Mae, but she sounded tempted. "Now, get out of here." She laughed. "Besides, I think Mine would be jealous if anyone sat up next to you."

Murphy ruffled Mine's ears. "Oh, he could take a back seat if he had to."

Mae turned to the children and held her arms out wide. "Come on, everybody, it's time for school. We want to be able to show Father Parker how much we've learned since his last visit. Let's go."

Murphy watched the children stop playing and willingly follow Mae inside. They were good kids, he thought, every one of them—not stuck up and spoiled the way some of the kids in town were.

The mules knew the dusty old trail by heart. They picked their way over the stones. Murphy glanced up at the blackened scar on the mountainside by the stream. He saw shoots of bright purple fireweed, the first plant to grow back after the fire had taken root underneath the charred pines. Murphy wondered if he'd ever forget that fire at the prospecting camp.

There had been more children than usual around this camp. The children even had a school in a tent, and that's where Mae Woodward came in. She was their teacher. The night of the fire was Halloween night. Mae Woodward had organized a Halloween pageant for all the kids. Everyone in the camp was excited that night. A vein of gold had been discovered that day. Murphy remembered the thrill of finding the first big nugget.

Murphy couldn't look at the charred scar on the hill without thinking of Garrett. Garrett and greed. The two words even sounded as if they went together. Garrett owned almost all of Jackson City and most of the gold claims. That October, when he learned that gold had been discovered on land he didn't own, he sent his men in with dynamite. Murphy would never forget the horrible sound as sticks of dynamite were thrown right into the tents of the men and women who were resting after a hard day of panning—the sounds of the dying and the screams of the children as Murphy and Moses tried to protect them from the sight of their parents, blown apart. The only adults who survived were Murphy, Moses, and Mae Woodward. Murphy and Moses had been down at the stream, working late into the night. Mae and the children had been in the school tent a mile down the hill. All the children survived and were safe.

"Safe," Murphy muttered to himself as the wagon clattered along the road. How safe were they when the only thing keeping them from the workhouse was "Father" Murphy, the priest who wasn't a priest? If the authorities ever found out, Murphy knew exactly how safe the children would be.

And what about himself? Murphy knew he had to make some hard decisions about himself too. He couldn't just stay on, hiding in a priest's robes. Murphy had never been the kind of man to hide.

Murphy felt Mine's muzzle on his arm. The dog seemed to read Murphy's thoughts. Murphy rubbed Mine on his broad head.

7

"You thinking about Garrett, too, Mine?" Murphy said out loud, more to himself than to Mine. Murphy didn't think that Mine had a guilty conscience, even though Mine was responsible for Garrett's death. After the "accident" Murphy had gone into Garrett's saloon, blind with rage. He had called Garrett out of his office and told Garrett to his face that he had killed innocent people.

Garrett just kept stepping backward. He made a slight nod of his chin to his men, and suddenly two of them grabbed Murphy by the neck. It took six of Garrett's men to force Murphy out of the saloon—six against one.

Somehow, once he was back out in the street, Murphy lost his anger. He dusted himself off and was ready to leave, but Garrett wasn't finished. Murphy heard his name called from an alley. He could see the glint of a derringer in Garrett's hand.

"What's the matter? Cat got your tongue? You had plenty to say back there." Garrett sounded almost like a man of courage with a gun in his hand. Of course, Garrett knew that John Murphy never carried a gun.

"I got nothing more to say to you," said Murphy.

"You got nothing to say to anybody," said Garrett, raising the derringer and taking aim.

Murphy felt something whoosh by him at waist level. He heard a gun go off. He rushed into the alley to see Mine standing over Garrett. Somehow Mine had jumped on Garrett's shooting arm. In his struggle to shake off the dog, Garrett had fallen on his gun and shot himself in the stomach. He was dead in seconds.

Murphy shook his head, bringing himself back to the present. Garrett was dead. There was nothing he could do about that. But he had heard rumors that Garrett's brother was coming to town, seeking revenge for his brother's death, revenge against "Father" Murphy.

CHAPTER
··⟫ 2 ⟪··

In the middle of Jackson City a slim, elegant man, dressed in a black suit with a wine-colored brocade vest, carefully unpacked his possessions— leather-bound books with gold lettering stamped on the spines, a statue of a half-naked woman standing gracefully on one leg as if frozen in flight. The man caressed each possession as he took it out.

Another man entered the room, carrying a large box. "This is the last of it, Boss," said the newcomer. He was six foot three, almost as big as Murphy, but with small, mean eyes. "You know, you were right about that house. Awful big place for one man to rattle around in."

"I like living in town, Frank," said the man in the brocade vest. "My brother left everything to me. He would have wanted me to live here." The man looked around his new office with approval.

"They're putting up the new sign outside. You want to have a look?" said Frank.

The man nodded coolly and walked out onto the dusty main street. Three men were hoisting a newly painted sign that read, in black and gold letters, GARRETT'S SALOON AND GAMBLING HALL.

"What do you think, Boss?" Frank asked anxiously, but his boss wasn't looking at the sign. He was staring down the street at a mule wagon, a man, and a dog.

"That's Murphy," whispered Frank. "You know who he is, don't you? He's a big man. People around here say he was the only man your brother couldn't buy or push around."

"He can be cut down to size. I haven't met the man yet who couldn't be."

"I don't know . . . talk around town is that Murphy took your brother on and won."

"You find out everything you can about him. He's got a weak spot somewhere . . . and I want to know where."

Murphy glanced at Garrett as he rode by the saloon. He looked somewhat familiar, but Murphy didn't pay much attention to him. Up ahead Murphy saw an old friend, Ray Walker, working in the sawmill.

Murphy pulled back on the reins. "Whoa . . ." He looked down at his friend, who was covered with sawdust and sweat. "Working kind of hard for a newly married man, aren't you, Ray?" asked Murphy jovially. "I thought you'd be taking some time off."

Ray Walker picked up a long two-by-four and shoved it onto a pile. He seemed to be avoiding Murphy's eyes. "Oh . . . well," Walker stammered. "The orders are piling up. I . . . can't afford to get behind, you know."

Murphy was puzzled. Ordinarily Ray Walker was

11

the most open of men, but today he seemed troubled and certainly not eager to talk. Well, John Murphy was not a man to pry. He tightened the reins and got ready to move on.

"Ray, I won't keep you from your work," he said, "but why don't you bring your daughter and that new wife of yours out to Gold Hill for Sunday supper? Mae'd love to see you, I know."

"We'll do that," replied Walker politely.

"All right, we'll look for you." Murphy snapped the reins and the mules continued down the road to where the stagecoach had stopped.

Father Parker practically bounced off the stage, a big smile on his young, handsome face. He was an itinerant priest who traveled all over the Dakotas, and he was the only outsider who knew about Murphy's charade. Father Parker didn't approve of anyone pretending to be a priest, but he felt that the children at the orphanage came first. Besides, he liked Murphy and didn't have the heart to turn him in to the authorities.

"You certainly look happy about something," said Murphy as he helped Father Parker stow his bag in the back of the wagon.

"I am," said Father Parker.

"I know—you've figured out a way for me to stop pretending I'm a priest," said Murphy eagerly.

Father Parker grinned. "Let's just say that if all works according to plan, you may be able to go back to being just plain old John Murphy."

"Hallelujah!" shouted Murphy.

Father Parker smiled. "That's an appropriate response from an almost priest."

"Tell me about it," said Murphy.

Father Parker shook his head. "Let's wait till we get to Gold Hill. I want to tell you, Mae, and Moses all together."

By the time Murphy and Father Parker got back to Gold Hill, it was almost dusk. They walked in on Mae and Moses, who were studying a piece of paper on the table.

"Is this the front door?" Mae asked Moses, not realizing that Father Parker and Murphy had arrived.

"Yes," answered Moses. "And I figure we can put my bed in one room . . . and Murphy's bed over here . . ."

"Hello!" shouted Father Parker.

Mae looked up from the drawing and smiled. "Father Parker! Welcome back!"

"What was that I heard about putting Murphy's bed somewhere?" said Murphy. "Murphy's bed doesn't go anywhere before it asks Murphy."

Moses laughed. "Don't get all riled up. I had a good idea. As long as we're living in a ghost town, we might as well make use of more than one building. I thought I'd fix up the abandoned company store building for us. It wouldn't be nearly as crowded as the loft. You wouldn't have to bump your head when you stood up . . . and I wouldn't have to listen to Mine snore."

"Mine doesn't snore," said Murphy. "He is simply a dog that likes to let you know he's asleep."

13

"He snores," said Moses, turning to Father Parker. "Father Parker, we can leave your bed up in the loft. It will give you a little privacy during your stay with us."

"I'm not going to be staying in Gold Hill anymore," said Father Parker. "You won't have to worry about me."

"What are you talking about?" objected Mae. "You know you're always welcome here."

"Bishop Shay has given me authorization to build a church in Jackson City. I'm going to have my own parish!"

"Oh, that's wonderful," said Mae, opening her arms and hugging Father Parker.

Moses clapped Father Parker on the back. "No more dragging around from town to town."

"So that's your secret," said Murphy. He didn't sound quite as thrilled as the others. "But I don't see how that will save these children from Claymore, or how it will get me out of my charade."

"I'll explain," said Father Parker. "You see, once we have an official church in Jackson, I am sure I can get the parish to take over the financial responsibility for the school. Rodman will have no authority over the children once we have a real church in town. In fact, I'm going into Jackson tomorrow to start looking for some land."

Murphy's eyes lit up. "Now, that's what I call really good news. I can get out of these priest's robes and back to my real life." Murphy was so happy that he didn't notice the quick look of hurt that flashed across Mae Woodward's eyes.

CHAPTER
⋯⋐ 3 ⋑⋯

Back in Jackson City a woman Mae Woodward's age paced up and down in her living room. It was a small room, built above the sawmill. Nothing in it was as fancy as the objects in Garrett's office, but everything looked as if it had been chosen with care and love. The furniture gleamed from layers of wax, and the few good dishes, white china with blue flowers twined around the edges, were carefully displayed. Every few seconds the woman looked at the door hopefully. Once or twice she paused in front of the door, started to open it, and then changed her mind. She looked out the one window in the room at the dark street and then turned again.

Finally the door opened. A girl stood there, her bonnet carelessly thrown off her head. She was about fourteen, and she had a dark, brooding look about her. Her face was broad, and her figure was full but not plump. She had lost most of her baby fat. She would have been pretty except for the pout on her mouth.

"Emma!" cried the woman.

The girl ignored her.

"Emma, where have you been?" demanded the

woman. "I've been worried about you. Your father told you to let me know if you were staying out after dark. Emma! I need to know if you're all right."

"Madeline, you don't need to know anything about me," said Emma coolly. "I'll do as I please and you can't stop me."

Madeline tried to control her anger. She reminded herself for the thousandth time that Emma was her stepchild. Madeline felt it was up to her to bridge the widening gap between them. Emma was Ray Walker's only child, and her mother had died when Emma was just a baby. Until Ray Walker had met Madeline, Emma and her father had lived alone. Emma didn't like sharing her father with anyone.

Madeline put her hands gently on Emma's shoulders and tried to make the girl look at her.

"Emma, can't you believe that I care about you? I . . . worry about you, alone out in the dark. I get concerned about you."

Emma shrugged her shoulders so violently that Madeline's hands flew up. "Concerned?" mocked Emma. "The only thing you've concerned yourself with is taking my father away from me."

Madeline felt as if she had been punched in the stomach. "How can you say that!" she cried.

"You know it's true," said Emma. She didn't raise her voice, but Madeline felt the girl's hatred and it made her cringe.

"Emma, if we're going to live together in this house, we have to get along."

Emma moved to the other side of the room. Her

back was to the door and she didn't see her father enter. "I don't want to live with you. Why don't you just go away!"

"Emma!" shouted Ray Walker. His voice was choked with shock.

Emma turned to her father. "Well, it's true, isn't it? She's not my mother and she'll never be my mother. We were fine before she came here." Emma's eyes focused on a framed picture, standing in a place of honor on a table. The silver frame was so highly polished that it gleamed in the light from the oil lamps. Madeline and Ray Walker stood stiffly in the photo, a portrait of their wedding day.

Emma seized the silver frame and flung it to the floor. Shards of glass exploded across the room. "Why don't you just go away, Madeline?" Emma yelled. "Just go away!" Emma ran into her room and slammed the door.

Ray Walker picked up his wedding photo. "It's just the glass. I can replace that for you."

Madeline held the photo in her hand and stared at it. "It's not that . . . I don't care about that. It's just that I've done everything I can to make her like me. I've been patient with her. I tried ignoring her bad behavior. I even tried yelling at her . . . but nothing works."

"She'll come around. It'll just take a little longer." Ray put his arms around his wife.

"I don't know, Raymond, I don't know. I wonder sometimes if we haven't made a mistake. Maybe we should never have gotten married."

17

Ray held her tightly. "I won't have you even thinking that." Madeline sighed. She loved Ray Walker so much and she wanted to love his daughter too. If only Emma would meet her, even a quarter of the way.

"I'm going in to talk to Emma," Ray said. "I'll make her understand that nothing she says or does will make me give you up. She's got to learn that I love you and I love her. One doesn't take away from the other. I'll go talk to her and then we can sit down and have a nice family supper together. It smells good."

Madeline dried her tears. She smiled up at her husband. "I'll put supper on the table."

Walker went into his daughter's room. The white chenille bedspread looked untouched. The window in Emma's room was wide open. The blue curtains that Madeline had made for Emma fluttered in the breeze. Emma had escaped through the window before, clinging to the drainpipe until she got a foothold on the balcony below.

Walker punched the wall in frustration. He ran out of his daughter's room. "She's run away again."

"Oh, no!" cried Madeline.

"She can't have gotten far. I'll be back just as soon as I've found her."

Walker rushed down the steps. The town was steeped in darkness. He called out, "Em . . . Em, honey!" He felt his heart pumping fast. He hated the fights between his daughter and Madeline. When he'd fallen in love with Madeline, he had pictured the three of them living together, full of love and happiness. He thought that Madeline would bring laughter into their lonely house—but it hadn't worked out that way, he had to admit to himself. Emma rarely laughed anymore.

The only sounds in the night came from Garrett's saloon. Walker could hear laughter in there, all right—men laughing because their bellies were full of liquor. And he could hear the high, shrill laughter of the dancing girls that Garrett had brought to town. Then he heard a softer laugh that sounded familiar. His heart froze. He swung open the doors of the saloon.

Emma's bonnet was thrown back off her head, and her dark hair flew as a drunken miner swung her around. The miner held Emma tight at the waist, and Emma's face was flushed.

Walker strode into the middle of the room and tore Emma away from the miner.

"Hey, it ain't your turn!" shouted the miner, keeping his arm firmly around Emma's waist.

"She's my daughter," said Walker as he wrenched the miner's arm away.

"Well, we were just dancing with her," said the miner.

For the first time Walker noticed the other men leering and laughing.

"Sure, she came in here and said she wanted to dance," said another of the miners.

Emma's father grabbed her firmly by the arm and began to push his way out. Garrett was leaning on the bar, a thin smile on his face. He was dressed in a beautiful cream-colored suit and a gray silk vest. He winked at Emma.

"Garrett, you shouldn't allow children in the saloon," said Walker angrily.

Garrett's smile didn't change. Lazily he let his eyes travel over Emma's body. Then his grin widened. "Don't look much like a child to me," he said and winked at Emma again.

Walker shoved Emma out of the saloon. He was so angry he was afraid that he would hit her. He dragged her to an alleyway behind the saloon and shook her by the shoulders. "Emma, I want you to come home, and I want you to apologize to Madeline for the terrible things you said to her tonight."

"I will not!" said Emma defiantly.

"Emma, Madeline loves you very much."

"I don't care." Emma nonchalantly tried to tie her bonnet under her chin. Inside she was shaking like a leaf. "You married her . . . I didn't!" she suddenly shouted. Then she lowered her voice. "You can force me to go back to *your* home, but I'll just run away again."

Walker winced when Emma said "your" home; she was telling him that she no longer considered it *her* home. He studied his daughter's stubborn jaw, so like his own.

"All right," he said. "I can't force you to live with me if you don't want to. But I won't have you running around the streets of Jackson like some—" Ray Walker stopped. He couldn't call his daughter the

20

name that had come to his lips, the name for the sort of women in Garrett's saloon. Instead he picked Emma up and threw her over his shoulder.

"What are you doing? Where are you taking me?" cried Emma, tears springing to her eyes, but her father didn't see them. He carried her to his wagon, dumped her in, and drove off.

CHAPTER
⌁ 4 ⌁

Emma's father didn't utter one word to her as they drove out of town. Emma thought of jumping off the wagon and running far away, but the truth was that she didn't know where to go. The men in the saloon had frightened her, much as she didn't like to admit it.

Emma wondered where her father was taking her. They passed the last homestead in town, and now they were out on a deserted, rocky road.

The stars were bright. The air had turned cold and Emma shivered in her thin dress. Was her father so angry with her that he was going to take her out into the wilderness and dump her? Was he just going to leave her there to survive on her own? Was he hoping a grizzly would get her or that she'd be massacred by Indians?

Emma shivered even more. Her father grunted and handed her an old horse blanket. Emma wanted to refuse it, but she was too cold. She wrapped the blanket around her shoulders. "Thank you," she said haughtily.

Her father only grunted again.

Emma must have dozed off, because she woke up with her head on her father's shoulder. His arm was around her, holding her steady. Emma breathed in his warm, familiar scent. She wished that she could ride alone with him like this forever. For a second her heart soared. Perhaps she and her father would leave Madeline behind and start a new life in a new town. Maybe they were going to Colorado, or even as far as California. Emma knew that lots of people picked up and disappeared every day from Jackson City, moving farther west. Maybe her father was taking her west, just her.

Emma looked up and noticed a group of forlorn-looking buildings standing in a clearing. It looked like a ghost town, except for a low light shining from one of the windows. Her father turned the wagon toward the ghost town.

"Where are we?" asked Emma.

"Gold Hill," answered her father.

"Gold? It sure doesn't look like much."

"The mine ran dry. It was a town out here before you were born. Now the only thing left is the old saloon and a few outbuildings. But it didn't stay a ghost town for long. This is where Mae Woodward runs her school."

"School! You're not going to leave me here with a bunch of babies. I know about that school . . . it's where those orphans live . . . they're *children*!"

"So are you," answered Emma's father curtly as he pulled the wagon to a stop.

Emma's father took her by the arm and pushed

her roughly out of the wagon. Emma pulled the blanket tighter around her shoulders and willed herself not to cry.

The door opened, and in the half-light from the oil lamps inside was the biggest man Emma had ever seen. He seemed to fill the doorway with his shoulders.

"John," said her father, "it's me, Ray Walker. I need your help."

John Murphy looked down at the girl deposited on the doorstep, a girl with dark, almost black eyes and a defiant look on her face, even though she was wrapped in an old horse blanket.

"Come on in, Ray," said Murphy. He stepped out of the way as Emma and her father walked in. Emma looked around the room. Half of it seemed to be a dining room and half a schoolroom. There were no children there, just Moses Gage, Mae Woodward, Murphy, and a young priest. Emma looked back at John Murphy. She liked the way the oil lamps caught the red highlights in his hair.

"You know my daughter, Emma, don't you?" asked Ray.

Murphy nodded slowly. "I almost didn't recognize her. She's gotten so grown-up."

Emma was pleased that he had noticed she wasn't a child.

Mae Woodward went to the stove and brought over a pot of coffee. "Sit down and warm yourselves." She poured a cup of coffee for Walker and handed Emma a fresh biscuit. "Here you are, Emma. This is freshly made tonight."

"Thank you, ma'am," said Emma politely, but already she could tell that she wasn't going to like Mae Woodward. She seemed so much like Madeline, nice on the outside . . . but Emma was sure that Mae Woodward didn't like her and couldn't be trusted.

Emma watched her father as he twisted his hat. She knew he was nervous and somehow she was glad, glad that he was nervous about dumping her in this place with a bunch of orphans.

Emma's father took a sip of the hot black coffee and sighed. "I've come to ask you if you'll take Emma for a while. I might as well speak in front of her. She knows why she's here." Walker looked meaningfully at Emma. She met his gaze but then dropped her eyes.

"Tonight was the fifth time she's run away from home since Madeline and I were married. I found her in Garrett's saloon. Next time I . . . I might not be able to find her. You've done such wonderful things with the children out here . . . I thought . . . maybe . . . you could reach her."

Moses looked hard at Emma but addressed his question to her father. "What makes you think she won't run away from us?"

"Well, out here, away from her friends in town, I think she'll settle down . . . and it's a long way to run away anywhere. I'll make a contribution to cover the expenses of her being here."

"What do you think about staying out here, Emma?" Mae asked kindly.

"It looks like I don't have much of a choice," said Emma.

"There's always a choice," said Mae softly, but Emma didn't hear her. She was staring at John Murphy, who was smiling at her.

"We'll be happy to take her, Ray," said Murphy. "I'm sure it won't be long before she's ready to come home to you and Madeline."

Emma wanted to tell John Murphy not to make any bets on it. She didn't realize that she was pouting again. Murphy thought her pout made her look about ten years old.

"Come on, Emma. You must be exhausted," said Mae. "Why don't you come upstairs with me. I'll show you your bed. The other children have just gone to sleep, but you'll meet them in the morning. I'm sure you'll make good friends here. We'll give you a room of your own right now."

"I'll be back in a little while with some of your clothes," said her father. He took a step toward her as if to hug her, but Emma kept her back ramrod stiff and followed Mae up the staircase.

As she went up the stairs Emma heard John Murphy say, "Don't worry, Ray, she'll be fine." Emma decided she liked the sound of John Murphy's low voice.

CHAPTER
❧ 5 ❧

In the morning Emma met the others. All the orphans at the school were children compared to her. Oh, a couple of them, like Will Adams and Lizette Winkler, looked to be nearly her age, at least chronologically. But Emma had always felt older than her years.

She didn't particularly like the children at the school. They seemed to be such goody-goodies, always looking for Mae and Murphy's approval. At breakfast Emma had pushed two kids out of the way so that she could sit next to Murphy.

Murphy hadn't talked much at breakfast. He'd said "Good morning" and then stared into his coffee cup. Emma had been happy just to sit next to him. She liked to look at his strong arms as he rested his elbows on the table. Besides, later in the day Mae Woodward had promised them all a picnic, and Emma knew that John Murphy was coming along. Perhaps on the picnic she'd find a way to be alone with him and make him notice her.

Meanwhile, Emma sat through Mae Woodward's lessons, staring out the window, hoping to catch a glimpse of John Murphy. This school was even smaller than her school in town. Of course, it wasn't divided into classes. The older children were supposed to help the younger ones, but Emma thought it wasn't her business whether the little kids learned to read or not.

Finally it was recess. "Do you want to play catch, Emma?" asked Ephraim Winkler. Ephraim was nearly twelve, but he looked younger because he was small. His dark eyes shone with intelligence. Like the rest of the children, his eyes sometimes clouded over when he thought of his parents, dead less than a year, but he had adjusted to the tragedy better than some of the others.

"Catch is for babies," said Emma. "Is that all you kids do during recess?"

"What did you do in town?" asked Ephraim. "I mean for recess."

Emma thought a minute. She felt in her pocket, glad to see that she had her pouch with her. She would teach these country kids a thing or two. "Come on with me," said Emma. "Someplace where Miss Woodward won't find us. I'll show you what we do in town."

"Hey, Will," called Ephraim. "Come on over here. Emma's gonna show us something."

"What's that?" asked Will skeptically. Will was older than the other children and reminded Emma a little of herself. She felt that he was challenging her. Well, she'd show him.

"Come on," said Emma. "Any of you can come . . . any of you who aren't afraid, that is."

About half a dozen children followed Emma. Ephraim took them to a hollow behind the main house. A group of cottonwood trees shielded the hollow from any prying eyes.

Emma sat down cross-legged on the grass. She pulled out the leather pouch and took out a packet of thin white papers.

She held one of the papers expertly between her thumb and forefinger and poured some tobacco into it from her pouch. Will and Ephraim watched her carefully.

"You just put about this much in the paper," explained Emma. "You roll it up like this." She rolled the paper, using her thumb to keep it round. Then she licked the edge to make it stick.

Just then Lizette found them and pushed aside one of the cottonwood branches. "What are you doing?" she asked. Lizette seemed to be about Emma's age, but she was the exact opposite of Emma in looks. She had long blonde hair, high cheekbones, and a delicate look about her, as if her skin were made of porcelain. She and Ephraim were brother and sister, though Ephraim was dark and looked more like Emma.

"Emma's showing us how to make a cigarette," whispered Ephraim.

Emma gave the cigarette a final lick and held it out to Ephraim. "Do you want to smoke it?" she asked him.

Ephraim backed away from the cigarette as if it were a snake. He had never smoked in his life, but he didn't want Emma to know that.

"What's the matter?" asked Emma as she offered the cigarette around. Nobody took it. "Are you all scaredy cats?"

"We are not!" exclaimed Will.

Emma passed the cigarette to Will. "Well, then, why don't you smoke it?" she asked.

"No," said Will slowly. "I . . . I . . ." Will stammered as he tried to think of an excuse.

"Nobody should smoke it," said Lizette. "It's not allowed."

"Well, who's going to know unless you tell?" asked Emma.

"You're not going to tell, are you, Lizette?" pleaded Ephraim, who didn't want anyone to get in trouble.

"She doesn't have to," said a voice. Mae Woodward pushed aside the cottonwood branches. "When none of you showed up after recess, I went looking for you."

Quickly Emma tried to hide the cigarette in her hand.

"Give that to me, Emma," Mae demanded.

"No, it's mine. You can't tell me what to do."

Mae took a step forward and grabbed the cigarette from Emma's hand. "Oh yes, I can tell you what to do. If you're going to live here, you'll abide by the rules just like everybody else."

Mae tore the cigarette to shreds and ground the tobacco into the dirt. "I have always thought that if you have to sneak off to do something, it's probably something you shouldn't be doing."

Ephraim looked up at her soulfully. "Does this

mean we're not going on the picnic with you and Mr. Murphy?''

"No," answered Mae. "I promised you a picnic after your chores and I think we should still go. But I don't want this ever to happen again. Is that understood?"

"Yes, ma'am," said all the children except Emma. Emma stood up and brushed off a few strands of tobacco that had stuck to her dress. She walked away from Mae without a word.

"Get started on your chores now," said Mae, watching Emma go.

Lizette hung back until the other children had left. She turned to Mae. "What are you going to do about Emma?" Lizette asked.

"What do you mean?" Mae shielded her eyes from the sun, trying to see where Emma had gone.

"She was pushing everybody around at breakfast," explained Lizette. "She won't hardly talk, and when she does, she says something mean."

Mae put her arm around Lizette's shoulder as they walked. "It's kind of hard having her around, isn't it?" asked Mae.

Lizette nodded. She didn't like to tattle, but Emma *was* mean. She scared Lizette.

Mae thought hard, trying to find the right words. She understood how Lizette felt. Life had been easier before Emma arrived, and Mae had a feeling that Emma wasn't through causing trouble.

"Lizette, this is a little hard to understand, maybe," said Mae. "But sometimes people are afraid that you're not going to like them, so they push you away first."

"Is that what Emma's doing?" asked Lizette.

"Yes, I think so. Try and give her a little more time, all right? Now, go do your chores so you'll be done in time for the picnic."

Mae was more worried about Emma than she had let on to Lizette. Emma seemed so sullen and unhappy, and Mae hoped the child wouldn't run away. Mae laughed a little to herself for calling Emma a child. Emma wasn't a child. She was something in between—not a child anymore, but certainly not yet a woman.

Mae went up to Emma's room and found her stuffing her clothes into her carpetbag.

"What are you doing?" asked Mae.

"Aren't you going to send me away?" asked Emma.

"No," said Mae. She sat on the bed and began to take Emma's things out of the carpetbag.

"Aren't you even going to punish me?" asked Emma. She jutted her chin out. Mae could see that she was close to tears.

"It seems to me that you're doing a real good job of punishing yourself," said Mae gently as she unpacked the rest of Emma's things. "Emma, we want you to stay. We want you to be happy. But you have got to try a little harder to meet us halfway."

Emma looked at Mae suspiciously. Part of Emma wanted to cry her heart out on Mae's shoulder, and part of her hated Mae for making her feel as if she understood. Emma knew that nobody understood how she felt. Nobody ever had and nobody ever would.

Mae saw the stubborn look come across Emma's face and stood up. At least she had tried. "Come on, Emma, put these things away," said Mae. "Then come down and help with the picnic baskets."

CHAPTER
·◦ᢧ 6 ᢙ◦·

While Mae prepared for the picnic, Father Parker and Moses got ready to go to town to buy some property for a church.

"Are you sure you don't want me to go with you?" asked Murphy.

"John, you and Mae go on that picnic," said Moses. He winked at Father Parker.

"Come on, Moses," said Father Parker. "Stop teasing the poor man."

"I don't know what you two are talking about," said Murphy huffily. But he knew. He realized that Moses had guessed how he had begun to feel about Mae Woodward. Murphy had never thought of himself as a romantic man. Loners didn't have romances with someone as good and sweet as Mae. Murphy's feelings puzzled him and he wondered how long he could stay at Gold Hill without Mae guessing how he felt.

When Moses and Father Parker arrived in Jackson City, Father Parker went to the register's office for a list of properties for sale. He brought it back out to the wagon. "Look, Moses," he said excitedly.

"There's an old school for sale right in town. Let's go look at that first."

"Fine with me," said Moses. "But better wait until you see it. You look like you're about to buy it sight unseen."

Father Parker gave an embarrassed laugh. "You're right, Moses. It's just that I'm so excited about having my own church. If I can find the right building, the bishop will be pleased. And if he's pleased, I'm sure I can convince him to let the church take over Gold Hill. Murphy won't have to pretend he's a priest anymore."

"You'll get your church, Father," said Moses.

They drove to the property. Father Parker leaped off the wagon. The abandoned school building was a large wooden rectangle. Even Moses had to admit that it would be ideal for a church.

A middle-aged man with a kindly face was standing on the steps of the building about to post a notice.

"Hello!" shouted Father Parker. "I'm looking for Mr. Spencer Nelson."

"That's me," said the man. "What can I do for you, Father?"

"I understand that this property is for sale."

"That's right. Public auction's this Saturday. I was just posting the notice."

Father Parker eyed the building longingly. "Ahh . . . it's just perfect for us."

Mr. Nelson smiled at the priest's enthusiasm. "You're planning to start a school, are you?"

35

"No . . . a church," said Father Parker hesitantly. He knew that some people in frontier towns objected to permanent Catholic churches.

"A church!" exclaimed Mr. Nelson. "Well, sir, I'm a God-fearing man myself, and that's the truth. I tell you, nothing would make me prouder than to know that a church was standing on a piece of property I used to own."

"I'm glad to hear that," said Father Parker.

"But, uh, you have to understand, Father," stammered Mr. Nelson, suddenly looking very embarrassed. "I'm going to have to sell it to the highest bidder."

"Oh, of course," said Father Parker. "Would you mind telling me what you hope to get?"

"Well, I'd be more than satisfied with a hundred dollars," said Mr. Nelson.

Moses put a hand on Father Parker's shoulder to keep him from blurting out that a hundred dollars was exactly what the bishop had given him.

"Would you mind if we looked around?" Moses asked.

"Oh, no, sir, go ahead. Help yourself."

As they went inside Moses noticed a stranger, a rather smooth and citified stranger at that, staring up at the building.

"Public auction's next Saturday, friend," said Mr. Nelson to the stranger. The stranger nodded, but he seemed more interested in Moses and Father Parker than in the building.

❊   ❊   ❊

Later that day Garrett was sitting in his office in the back of his saloon when Frank, his six-foot-three bodyguard, knocked on the door.

"I think I got something for you, Boss," said Frank.

Garrett leaned forward eagerly and put his elbows on the desk. "On John Murphy?" he asked.

"Word in town is that he had something to do with your brother's death. Folks say it was an accident, though. Your brother went after Murphy with a gun and Murphy's dog jumped up and made the gun go off."

"I knew all that before I got here," said Garrett disgustedly. He leaned back in his chair and put his feet on the desk. He picked up a Mexican knife and began to clean his nails with the edge of the long silver blade. "What else have you found out, Frank?" he asked. "It better be good, considering what I pay you."

"There's a priest who's Murphy's friend . . . Father Parker. He's one of those traveling priests, you know, a young guy. He comes here every month or so for a day or two."

"What about him?" asked Garrett, sounding bored.

"He's looking to build a church in Jackson."

"So? What does that have to do with the price of beans?"

"It might have something to do with the money in your pocket," said Frank. "We've got an ordinance in this town. It says that once you build a church, you can't have a saloon open on Sundays."

Garrett looked interested. "Sunday is one of my

best days. Miners and cowboys like to get drunk on Saturday night and stay drunk. They lose a lot gambling on Sundays."

"I know, Boss," said Frank smugly, as if glad that Garrett would have a little problem on his hands.

Garrett pointed his silver dagger at Frank. "We'll just have to make sure that he doesn't get his church, won't we?" he said.

He stared into space, almost forgetting that Frank was in the room. Finally he spoke again. "I'll take care of the church. You stay on Murphy. I want to know every dirty piece of gossip you can dig up about him. I want something I can *use*!"

CHAPTER

⋯⊰ 7 ⊱⋯

If Garrett could have seen John Murphy at that moment, he would have despaired about ever getting any "dirty gossip" on him. Murphy lay in the sun in a field of wildflowers, surrounded by children. Mae Woodward sat just a few feet from him. Murphy thought to himself that he had never felt so contented. They had eaten the fried chicken and zucchini bread that the children and Mae had made. It had all been delicious. Now John Murphy felt like he could laze in the sun forever.

The children, however, being children, were not as content to lie still. "Miss Woodward," asked Ephraim, "can we go climbing?" Ephraim pointed to a rocky trail that led to some overhanging cliffs.

"Yes," said Mae, "but be careful."

"All right!" cried Ephraim excitedly.

"We'll be careful," said Lizette.

"Come on, everybody, let's go," said Ephraim, bolting up the trail. The rest of the children followed him. Lizette noticed Emma leaning on the wagon by herself. She recalled her talk with Mae that morning and decided to try harder to make Emma feel wanted.

"Do you want to come climbing with us?" asked Lizette. "It's beautiful up there. There are loads of wildflowers."

"You've seen one wildflower, you've seen them all," said Emma. She glanced over at John Murphy. He was sitting up and talking to Mae Woodward. Emma wished that *she* could be alone with John Murphy, but Mae Woodward just didn't seem to know when she wasn't wanted. Emma decided that she might as well go exploring. "I'll go," said Emma.

"Good," said Lizette. "Come on, I'll show you some beautiful flowers."

"Now be careful," said Murphy, turning around to watch them go. Emma gave him her most dazzling smile.

Mae stretched out her arms. It felt so good to just rest in the sun, yet now that she and John were alone, she felt shy. Mae got to her feet.

"I guess I'll start packing up."

Murphy grabbed her hand. "It'll keep, Mae." He pulled her back down to the grass beside him. "You said we were coming out here on this picnic to relax and have a good time. You can take a minute to do that yourself, you know."

"You're right," said Mae. She lay down on the grass and looked up at the sun on the hills. "Oh, I can't believe that Moses would rather go into town than come out here with us. It's such a beautiful day!"

"Yes, it is," agreed Murphy, "but he's like a kid

with a new toy. All he can talk about is moving into that company store."

Mae laughed. "Father Parker and Moses are like two peas in a pod . . . they're both so excited about their new projects."

"They're both good ideas," said Murphy. "I'm surprised Moses and I didn't think about fixing up the company store before. I guess I just never thought the two of us'd be staying in the loft that long."

Mae glanced at Murphy. She kept quiet. She knew that this was a long speech for Murphy. He wasn't much of a man for saying what was on his mind.

"It's kind of funny," continued Murphy. "It's funny how you find yourself settling into a place before you even know it's happened."

"Are you sorry about that?" Mae asked.

"About what?"

"Settling in," Mae said softly.

Murphy smiled at her. "No, no," he said quickly. "A little surprised, maybe, but never sorry."

Meanwhile, the children were at the top of the cliffs. Emma peered over the ledge. The other children stood a foot or two back. "Emma, you shouldn't go so close to the edge," warned Lizette.

Emma glanced back at Lizette and gave her a dirty look. " 'Emma, you shouldn't go so close to the edge,' " she mocked, imitating Lizette's voice perfectly. "You're such a goody-goody." Emma looked over the ledge again. About twenty feet down the slope a bunch of daisies grew out from around a rock.

"Ephraim, I betcha can't pick those flowers," challenged Emma.

"What flowers?" asked Ephraim, coming closer to the edge.

"You see them?" said Emma. She pointed down. "Those flowers!"

"Those are just weeds," said Ephraim, taking a step back from the cliff.

"I knew you'd be scared," sneered Emma.

"I am not!" protested Ephraim, but he didn't step closer to the cliff.

"Here, hold this," said Emma, taking off her bonnet. She looked down the cliff for a foothold. Then she grabbed a branch of an aspen tree and began to let herself down the side.

"Emma!" shouted Lizette. "I don't think you'd better."

Emma let go of the branch and slid down the rest of the way to the flowers.

"Emma, please!" pleaded Lizette.

"It was nothing," said Emma. "Anybody with guts could do it."

Emma reached over to pick some of the daisies. Suddenly her foot slipped. She tried to grab on to something. Her hand gripped the daisies, but they came out by the roots. Emma tumbled down the cliff, bouncing from rock to rock. She screamed as the rocks tore her dress. She tried to stop but instead rolled faster and faster.

"Emma!" yelled Lizette.

The cliff was on two levels. The first level Emma

was tumbling down was not really all that steep. But the second level was more like a sheer rock slide. From up above, the children could see that if Emma didn't stop before the second level, she would fall to her death.

Emma could feel her speed gathering as her body hurtled downward. She felt as if time were standing still. Although she knew she was falling faster, everything felt slowed down. She saw every rock as she bounced off it. She saw a small tree hanging out over the second ledge of the cliff. Desperately she flung her hands out and grabbed for a branch.

The tree caught the weight of her body and her legs hung down beneath her. Emma sobbed as she tried to hold on.

"Emma, are you all right?" shouted Ephraim.

"I'll go down and get her," said Will, starting down the ledge.

Lizette grabbed Will's arm. "You can't. You'll fall too. Go get Mr. Murphy! He'll know what to do."

Will looked down at Emma. He realized that Lizette was right. Even if he reached Emma safely, he wasn't strong enough to carry her back up. "Just stay there, Emma!" shouted Will. "Hold on."

"Help me!" cried Emma.

"We're getting Mr. Murphy!" shouted Lizette. "You'll be all right."

"Help me, please," sobbed Emma. "Oh, God, help me."

Will ran along the edge of the cliff and then down the back to Mae and Murphy. They were involved in their conversation and didn't notice him. Will took a breath and gasped out, "Mr. Murphy! Come quick! It's Emma!"

Murphy and Mae turned toward Will. "What about Emma?" asked Murphy.

"She fell off the ledge," gasped Will. "It's a long way down and she can't get back up. She's hanging on to a tiny tree."

Mae's hand flew to her mouth. "Oh, my God," she whispered. She scrambled to her feet and ran toward the cliff.

"I'll get some rope." Murphy dashed to the wagon and coiled a long piece of rope around his shoulder. Then he took off after Mae and Will.

Lizette could see them approaching. "Hold on, Emma! They're coming!"

Emma didn't answer. She was using all her strength to hang on to the tree.

Murphy stared down the ledge. He could see the second sheer descent and he could hear the creek running below. He reckoned it was about two hundred yards to the bottom.

"Emma! I'll be right down there! Hang on!" shouted Murphy.

Murphy tied one end of the rope around a thick pine. Unlike the aspen tree's, the pine's roots went deep and Murphy knew that the tree would hold his weight.

Then he wrapped the loose end of the rope around his waist and inched his way down the cliff. He kept peering over his shoulder at Emma, fearful

44

that the rocks he was scattering with his descent might hit her.

"Hold on just a second, sweetheart," he crooned, the way he might talk to a frightened horse. He wanted to make sure that he was behind her before he took her weight. "Easy, easy, now. Just don't move . . . don't move. Let me get down to you."

Emma looked up at him. Her eyes were as big as saucers. Murphy reached her. He braced himself at the edge of the ledge and picked Emma up. He held her next to his chest. She was quivering all over. She buried her head in his chest and began to sob.

"Emma, Emma? Are you all right? Is anything broken?" asked Murphy softly.

"I'm so scared," Emma blurted out.

"Scared? Well, that's all right," said Murphy, keeping his arms around Emma. "Scared we can mend. It was a broken bone I was worried about."

Murphy tested the rope. It held firmly, but he knew that he couldn't risk putting their combined weight on it and pulling them up.

"Emma, we have to go down over this ledge to the creek. We can't get back up. You're going to have to be brave, but I'll hold you. Together we'll make it down, won't we?"

Emma nodded. If Murphy had asked her to jump over the cliff at that moment, she would have.

"All right," said Murphy. He wrapped the rope around her waist. "I want you to put your arm around me. Put your other arm on the rope. Cling to me like a monkey. Can you do it?"

Emma said, "Yep!"

Murphy smiled at her. "That's my girl. That's what I like to hear. We are a *team*. Okay, here we go."

With the girl's weight added to his own, Murphy prayed the rope would hold. He used his feet to take the weight off the rope and made his way slowly down the cliff. Loosened rocks careened to the bottom, but the rope held.

Emma clung to Murphy as if he were life itself. Finally they reached the bottom.

"She's all right!" Murphy shouted to Mae and the children.

He and Emma could hear the cheers echo in the canyon. Murphy unwrapped the rope from around Emma's waist. "We made it, sweetheart. You were very brave. Now we'll just follow the stream right back to our picnic site."

Emma's eyes gleamed. "First, Mr. Murphy, I'm going to kiss you." Emma reached up and flung her arms around Murphy's neck and kissed him on the cheek. Murphy laughed, happy that what could have been a disaster had turned out so well.

CHAPTER
·•⋊ 8 ⋉•·

On Saturday, the day of the auction, Murphy agreed to go into town with Father Parker. "You can pick up some things we need to fix up our new home," said Moses, taking out his pencil and adding more to his list.

"Moses, it'll take me all day just to carry that stuff out to the wagon," Murphy said with a laugh, but he took the list.

When they got to the site of the abandoned school building, a small crowd had already gathered. Father Parker shook his head. "I hope nobody's as set on this property as I am," he said as he jumped off the wagon.

"I don't think that would be possible," said Murphy, scanning the crowd. "I think most of these people are here just for the entertainment. I know most of them and none of them have much use for a building this size. You just relax. I'm going to the store to pick up that hardware for Moses. I'll come back and pick you up later."

"Mmm," said Father Parker, gazing intently at the building.

Murphy took the reins in his hand. "Good luck, Father," he said.

"Thanks, John. I'm sorry I've been in such a trance this morning."

"Just don't get in a trance and bid over your head," warned Murphy. He snapped the reins lightly on the mules' backs and rode off.

Father Parker moved to the front of the crowd. He tried to comfort himself with John Murphy's words. Most of the crowd did look as if they were just there for an afternoon of entertainment. A good auctioneer was almost worth an admission price.

Spencer Nelson, the owner of the building, stepped forward. "All right, friends, can I have your attention? Just gather around and we'll get started. Mr. Whitehead, here, is gonna lead the auction today."

A dapper-looking man in a plaid suit picked up the gavel. He had a small, neat, waxed mustache and wore a monocle in his right eye. He stepped up to the makeshift podium like a Shakespearean actor taking the stage.

> "Ladies and gentlemen, let's begin,
> Although this crowd's a trifle thin.
> I ask you all to pay attention.
> Time is money, need I mention.
> Raise your hand and speak your number.
> I will neither sleep nor slumber."

With each couplet the crowd laughed and seemed

to settle in for the fun. Mr. Whitehead adjusted his monocle with each laugh.

"Who'll bid a hundred just to open?
 I don't want less, but I know you're hopin'."

A well-dressed man in a dark brown suit raised his hand and said, "Twenty-five dollars."
Mr. Whitehead screwed his monocle into his eye.

"I have twenty-five and I now want fifty.
 Fifty's thrifty for a place this nifty."

A woman in the crowd nodded her head. The auctioneer smiled.

"She bid fifty and she's glad she did.
 Now, come on, folks, with a seventy-five.
 A bee wanting honey don't stay in the hive."

"Fifty-five," said Father Parker in a clear voice. It was his first bid.

"Fifty-five. That's all you bid.
 If I don't hear sixty, I'm gonna put on the lid."

"Sixty," said the well-dressed stranger.
"Sixty-five," answered Father Parker.
"Seventy-five," said the stranger quickly, even before the auctioneer had to ask for a higher bid.

"Seventy-five!
 Now this auction's looking alive!
 I want a hundred.
 I don't want this property plundered!"

The crowd soon realized that Father Parker and the well-dressed stranger were the two real contenders.

Father Parker felt his heart pound. He wanted that property so badly. "Uh, eighty dollars," he said.

"One hundred dollars," said the stranger in a strong, calm voice, as if that sum were nothing to him.

Father Parker felt the sweat running down his face. The bishop had given him orders not to spend more than a hundred dollars. Yet the school was so perfect. Surely God would provide another five dollars. "A hundred and five," said Father Parker, raising his hand.

The crowd gasped. Everyone, including the owner, knew the property wasn't worth any more than a hundred.

"One fifty!" said the stranger, looking over at Father Parker and giving him a tight-lipped smile.

Father Parker groaned to himself.

"A hundred and fifty, saint's alive . . .
Do I hear a hundred and seventy-five?"

The auctioneer looked at Father Parker. Father Parker shook his head. He knew the bishop would never forgive him if he spent money that the church didn't have.

"A hundred and fifty, once, twice, and thrice," said the auctioneer, pounding his gavel. "I tell you, folks, sales are nice. Sold! for a hundred and fifty dollars."

Father Parker watched as the stranger went up to Mr. Nelson and handed him a hundred and fifty dollars from a thick roll of bills. Minutes later Murphy drove up with the wagon.

"How did it go?" asked Murphy.

Father Parker turned. "I lost it, I'm afraid. Outbid by that man in the dark brown suit. Why anybody would want to spend a hundred and fifty dollars for that old building, I don't know."

"A hundred and fifty? That's kind of steep," said Murphy.

Father Parker blushed. "I got so carried away, I bid a hundred and five myself."

"Father, that's a lot of money!" exclaimed Murphy.

Father Parker smiled ruefully. "Especially since I only had a hundred." Father Parker took one last glance at the building as he climbed into the wagon. "Oh, well, there'll be other places, I suppose."

As Murphy and Father Parker drove out of town, the stranger in the dark brown suit made his way to Garrett's saloon.

He knocked on the door of Garrett's office and entered, taking the deed to the old school out of his pocket. "Here she is," said the stranger. "It cost you a hundred and fifty dollars. I still don't see why that building would be worth that much money to you."

"Were you bidding against a priest?" asked Garrett.

The stranger nodded. "He stayed in until the end."

Garrett smiled. "Well, let's just say that I have my reasons."

Garrett pulled a twenty-dollar bill from his wallet. "Here's another twenty for your trouble."

The stranger pocketed the money. "It sure is a pleasure doing business with you, Mr. Garrett."

CHAPTER

·-♦ 9 ♦·-

The Monday following the auction was a bright, sunny day out at Gold Hill. Moses crawled out on the roof of the old feed store and started hammering nails. Emma came out and gave him a big, warm smile.

"Good morning, Emma," said Moses.

"Glorious morning, isn't it?" said Emma. "Have you seen Mr. Murphy?"

"He's over by the blacksmith's shed," answered Moses, pointing with his hammer.

"Thanks!" shouted Emma. She skipped over to the shed, her feet barely touching the ground. Moses followed her with his eyes, smiling to himself.

Lizette stood in the center yard with a couple of the younger children, swinging a rope. "Emma, you want to jump rope with us?" she called.

Emma gave Lizette as big a smile as she had given Moses. "No, thanks," she said. "Maybe later." She ran on toward the blacksmith's shed.

Moses climbed down off the ladder to get another packet of nails. Mae walked over to say good morning.

"That Emma," said Moses. "She's like a different child these days."

Mae nodded and watched Emma round the corner. "I think the accident changed her. She just needed to know that someone cared about her. How's that roof coming along?"

"Oh, it should be done by tomorrow. Then I'm going to start on the inside. No sense in moving in until it's perfect."

Mae smiled at Moses. "You would say that," she teased.

Just then Matt, one of the children, threw a ball toward Mae. "Miss Woodward, catch!" he shouted.

Mae caught the ball expertly and threw it back overhand. "School will start in about five minutes!" she shouted. "But we've got time for a quick game of catch."

Meanwhile, over at the blacksmith's shed, Murphy was darning a horse blanket with a huge needle. Emma sat at his feet, staring at him.

Murphy felt uncomfortable with the girl's gaze, but he didn't know what to say to her. Emma was so easily hurt, and he was pleased that she was no longer so sullen.

He cut the thread with his teeth and then rethreaded the needle. He listened to the sound of Mae's laughter as she played with the children. "Emma," he said, "it seems to me you're spending most of your free time watching me do my work."

"Oh, I like it," said Emma. "It's fun."

"I bet you'd have more fun out there, playing with the others."

Emma shifted her position so that her ankles peeked out from beneath her skirt. She pretended to smooth out a wrinkle by her waist. "Naw . . . they're just children."

Murphy smiled to himself. "I see," he said gently. He went back to his darning.

"Mr. Murphy," said Emma hesitantly.

Murphy didn't look up. "Yep?"

"Do you think you'll ever get married?"

Murphy tried to hide his surprise at her question. "I—don't know," he stammered. "I couldn't really say."

"How do you know when you want to marry somebody?"

Murphy considered her question. It was a good one, he admitted, and not one that he had ever bothered to ask himself. He put down the horse blanket and looked at Emma seriously. "I never really thought about it," he said slowly, as if he were talking to himself. "I suppose when you want to be with a person more than anything in the world . . . and . . . well, when you can tell someone things about yourself you don't normally tell to people . . . that's when you'd think about getting married."

Emma seemed to catch only half of his words. Her mouth turned back into its familiar pout. "Nobody understands me. Nobody cares about me, either."

Murphy was brought out of his reverie about marriage. He had just realized that for the first time *he* felt that way about someone. He turned his thoughts back to Emma. "I think you're wrong about that, Emma. I think your father cares about you a great deal. And I think Madeline does too."

"Do you care about me?" Emma asked. Her heart began to pound as she waited for Murphy's answer.

"Of course I do," answered Murphy casually. He turned back to his horse blanket. He didn't see the look of absolute joy that crossed Emma's face.

Just then the school bell rang. Emma jumped up. "I'll see you after school!" she promised.

Murphy watched her go, but he was lost in his own thoughts about marriage.

At sunset Father Parker came galloping up on a horse, his robe flying behind him. He jumped off the saddle, his face aglow with excitement. "I found another place for the church!" he cried to Moses and Murphy, who were sitting on the porch with the children, watching the sun go down.

Moses laughed. "Lord, I thought you were going to tell us the War Between the States had started again."

Father Parker laughed at himself. "Well, I was pretty eager to tell you. It's the old feed store in town. It'll work out just fine. It's spacious, with a lot of windows. And there will be no auction. I shook hands with the owner. Tomorrow, when I give him the money, it's ours." Father Parker paused to take a breath. "Of course, it needs a lot of work on the inside."

Moses smiled at the young priest's enthusiasm. "We can help you with that, Father."

"Thanks," said Father Parker. "Once I sign the bill of sale, I'm going to take you up on that. Well, I'd better tend to my horse and let him cool off a little. Then I'm going to start drawing up some plans for remodeling."

Moses watched him go. He winked at Murphy. "Funny how a man can get all caught up in a building."

Murphy slapped Moses on the back and laughed so hard that all the children stared at him. Murphy couldn't stop laughing.

Moses waved to the children. "You go on now and get ready for bed. Murphy here just got something caught in his throat."

Emma watched them. She loved the way John Murphy laughed. She loved everything about John Murphy.

In class that afternoon Mae Woodward had read them some of the love sonnets of William Shakespeare. Emma thought about love. She knew that she belonged with John Murphy. She made it her business to know where he was every minute. She hoarded scraps of information about him the way prospectors hoarded gold. She liked to look at him when he didn't even know she was there.

Late that night she sat in her room and went over every movement that John Murphy had made. She remembered each word he had spoken to her that day. She stared into her oil lamp. Then she took out her inkwell and dipped in her feathered pen. Like William Shakespeare, she would give words to her love. She started to write. Suddenly the door to her room opened. Mae Woodward stood in the shadows. "Hey! Lights out was an hour ago," said Mae.

"I can't sleep," said Emma. She put her arms over the love poem.

"What are you working on?" asked Mae.

"Nothing," said Emma, slipping her poem under the blotter.

Mae looked at her kindly. She cupped Emma's chin with her hand. "Emma, I want you to know that I've been very pleased with you this last week. You keep up the good work and I think you're going to find yourself ready to get back home very soon."

Emma froze. "You're not going to send me home, are you?"

Mae could hear the fear in the girl's voice. "Well, no, not if you don't want to go. I just thought that when your father brought you here . . ."

"I won't go!" declared Emma passionately.

"All right, Emma," Mae said gently. "You can stay here as long as you want. But I do think it's time that you saw your father and had a talk with him. Otherwise, how are you going to know if you want to go home or not?"

"Maybe I'll never go back," said Emma. She didn't add the rest of her thoughts. Maybe she would marry John Murphy. Emma could just imagine her father's face when John Murphy confessed that he was in love with her. "She's not a child to me," John Murphy would say. Emma smiled at her thoughts. She didn't even notice that Mae Woodward had left the room.

CHAPTER
⋯∙◅ 10 ▻∙⋯

The next day Moses and Father Parker drove into Jackson City to purchase the feed-store building. All the way in Moses teased Father Parker about his elaborate plans for remodeling. But Moses stopped teasing as they came closer and saw flames rising high above the center of town. "A fire! Father, hurry," urged Moses.

Almost everyone in town had turned out with buckets to try to stop the blaze. Father Parker pulled the wagon to a halt. He jumped off and grabbed a bucket from a farmer and threw it on the blaze. "The church! My church!" cried Father Parker.

The farmer stared at him. "It's just the old feed store," he said. "It's hopeless. We're just trying to stop it from spreading. Give me that bucket. We need it to dampen down the other buildings."

Father Parker looked at Moses with despair. Together they watched the building burn. The roof caved in and flames licked the last of the corner timbers. Moses knew that the farmer was right. The building was doomed.

Moses put his hand on Father Parker's shoulder. "I

hate to say it, Father, but it's a lucky thing you didn't pay the man yesterday. Otherwise you'd be the proud owner of a burned-out building."

"Doesn't it strike you as more than a coincidence?" asked Father Parker angrily. "First I'm outbid, then the building I want to buy burns to the ground?"

Moses was a little shocked by the priest's outburst. "I think you're making more out of this than there is. Why would anyone want to do that to you?"

"I don't know. But I'm not going to stop until I get that church."

"I'm glad to hear that," said Moses.

They returned to Gold Hill and told Mae and Murphy about the fire. Murphy shook his head at their bad luck. "Maybe we should just buy a piece of land and go ahead and build the church ourselves."

"Well, we tried to find the owner of the feed store," said Moses. "We had just that idea in mind. But he disappeared right after the fire."

"It was very strange," added Father Parker. "It's like somebody forced him to leave town. Nobody would talk about it."

Murphy glanced at Moses. He wondered if Father Parker was so anxious to have his own church that he was imagining a conspiracy against him. But Moses nodded. "Father Parker's right. Something is suspicious."

"Tomorrow I'm going to make one last try," said Father Parker. "There's another small building, owned by George Williams. It's not perfect, but it

60

will do and at least he seems willing to sell. I've got to get a building by tomorrow. I'm supposed to report back to the bishop by the end of the week."

Suddenly Lizette burst into the room, out of breath. "A buggy's coming up the road. I think it's Mr. Rodman."

"Oh, no," groaned Murphy. "Here we go again." Murphy sprinted up the stairs to the loft. He opened the trunk where he kept his priest's robe and hurriedly put it on. Then he tied the belt around his waist. Moses helped him adjust the hood. "Well, let's go say hello to Rodman," said Moses.

Murphy sighed. "Moses, I can't tell you how much I hate this."

Moses made a final adjustment to Murphy's skirt. "Just wait until Father Parker gets settled in a church. He'll straighten out this whole mess. Meanwhile, think of the children."

Murphy nodded. He could hear Mae's voice downstairs. She sounded nervous. He climbed down, taking care not to trip on the long robe.

Murphy's mouth turned into an unaccustomed frown when he saw Rodman. How Murphy hated the man! Rodman's face was a pasty white, the color of a poisonous mushroom that never saw the sun. He was elegantly dressed in a perfectly tailored black suit that made the most of his knobby frame. Miss Tuttle, Rodman's assistant, looked like a dowdy pigeon from the city. She cooed and fluttered and bobbed her head up and down as she agreed with everything Rodman said.

"Good afternoon, Mr. Rodman," said Murphy from the top of the stairs.

"Good afternoon, Father Murphy," said Rodman with a slight nod. "I was just telling Miss Woodward that your files are not as they should be."

"Not at all correct," agreed Miss Tuttle, bobbing her head. "In addition to the financial statements you send in each month, the Territory requires a file on each child you take in."

"What kind of file?" asked Mae warily.

"Oh, we need to know the date of their arrival, their age, what happened to their parents, and . . . their legal guardian," tittered Miss Tuttle.

"The Church is the legal guardian for all of them," said Murphy emphatically.

Rodman's eyes narrowed. "I know," he said. "For now."

Murphy tried to control his temper. He wanted to shuck off his priest's robes and throttle Rodman. Rodman seemed to sense Murphy's hatred. He turned his back on Murphy and concentrated on Mae Woodward. "Miss Woodward, how long will it take you to prepare such a report?"

Mae glanced around the room. The children were staring at Rodman and Miss Tuttle like frightened animals. Mae kept her hands in her lap. She, too, felt like strangling Rodman. "I don't know. A few hours maybe. Would you like to wait?" she asked sweetly. She knew Rodman hated children, and the idea of having to sit in the same room with them for several hours would gall him.

Rodman pulled himself up to his full height, which still kept him more than a foot shorter than Murphy. "Miss Woodward," he said haughtily. "We have other business to attend to. We can't sit around here while you do your paperwork. You can bring it to the hotel in Jackson City when you're finished. We'll be staying in town a few days."

"Fine," answered Mae shortly. She rose and followed Rodman and Miss Tuttle to the door. Murphy kept his clenched fists hidden in his habit so that Rodman wouldn't see how angry he was.

"Good-bye, Father Murphy," said Rodman in his grating voice. "I hope the children appreciate the sacrifice you've made to be their legal guardian."

"It is not a sacrifice, but a joy," said Murphy. "A joy to see children grow up in sunshine and with love."

"Ah, yes," agreed Rodman. "We who have the vocation to take care of children are truly blessed."

Rodman and Miss Tuttle stepped up into the buggy and rode off.

Murphy swept the hood of his habit off his face. "The bloody hypocrite!" he muttered.

Mae didn't even bother to reproach Murphy for his language.

The children all stood outside and watched the buggy disappear. "I'm glad they didn't stay for supper," said Ephraim. "I hate it when they're here."

Emma was the only one who didn't watch the buggy. She was staring at John Murphy. "Why is Mr. Murphy wearing a priest's robe?" she asked.

63

"Mr. Rodman thinks he's a priest, like Father Parker," explained Ephraim. "It's the only way they let us keep the school. Otherwise we'd all have to go to the workhouse. Now, every time Rodman comes around, Mr. Murphy has to put on that priest's robe."

"What if they found out he was just pretending?" Emma asked thoughtfully.

"I don't know for sure," said Will. "They'd probably take him away and close down the school."

"Hmm," said Emma, lost in her own thoughts.

Later in the day, when everyone else was out doing chores, Emma took the poem she had written and sneaked up the stairs to the loft. Lovingly she put her poem down on Murphy's pillow. She rested her hand on Murphy's sheet. Everything that Murphy touched was precious to her.

The lid to Murphy's trunk was open. Emma saw the brown priest's robe lying in the trunk in a heap. Murphy had obviously thrown it there in a hurry after Rodman left. Emma picked up a corner of the robe and rubbed her cheek against it. She smiled to herself.

That evening Mae was working on her files by the light of the oil lamp. Her eyes hurt and her lower back ached from sitting in one position for too long.

She stretched and wondered what time it was. The moon was high over the mountain, and she knew that this time of year, the moon didn't rise until almost midnight.

She glanced up the stairs toward the loft and was surprised to see Murphy. He came down, carrying a piece of paper in his hand.

Mae smiled at him, secretly glad that he was still awake to share this quiet hour with her. She stood up and rubbed her hands on her back. "Well, I finally finished," she said.

"Good," said Murphy, looking over her shoulders at the long report.

"Everything the Territory could ever want to know about these children. All twenty of them. Oh, I had no idea it was going to take so long." Mae sat back down. Murphy sat beside her on the bench.

"Mae—uh—" Murphy stammered, not knowing how to begin.

"Is something wrong?" Mae asked anxiously.

Murphy thrust a piece of paper at her. "I think you'd better look at this. I found it on my bed."

Mae took the piece of paper.

"Your strong arms like the mighty birches have
    held me once.
Oh, that mine own arms could sing to tell you of
    my love. . . ."

Mae read the poem and then smiled. "Oh, I've been reading love sonnets to the children in class. This is lovely, especially considering that it's been written by a child."

"Emma?" guessed Murphy.

"It's her handwriting," said Mae. "Do you think she left this for you?"

"I'm afraid she did. She's been asking me a lot of strange questions lately, spending a lot of time around me. Oh, I should have seen this coming. I've just had so many things on my mind."

"Well, don't worry about it," said Mae. "You're just going to have to talk to her."

Murphy looked as if Mae were suggesting that he walk on water. "Mae, I can't do that. You know how I am with words. Can't you do it?"

Mae shook her head. "John, you are the only one who can talk to her about this. She'd think I was just interfering."

Murphy stared into the oil lamp. "I guess you're right." He looked out at the moon, now bright and full over the hill. The clouds passed across it, sending rays of moonlight shooting into the sky. Mae looked out the window with him. Murphy could hear her gentle breathing.

Neither of them noticed that Emma had sneaked down from her room and was huddled on the staircase. Emma couldn't sleep; she wanted to know what John Murphy would do when he found her poem. She held her breath and stood as still as a statue on the steps.

Murphy turned from the window. "Mae, there's someone else I should be talking to." Mae raised her eyes but kept silent. Murphy took her hand. "I think you know how I feel about you. I think maybe you knew before I did. My life just hasn't been the same since I met you . . . and I don't think it ever will be again."

Mae caught her breath. Finally, after all these months, she was hearing the words she had longed for. "John . . ."

Murphy looked at her, her fair hair and her wide eyes . . . the face he had come to love. He pulled her toward him. "Oh, Mae, I know there's a way that this is supposed to be said and everything, but, hang it . . . I just . . ." Murphy bent his head down and kissed Mae full on the lips.

Neither of them heard the quiet sob on the stairs as Emma covered her mouth to keep herself from crying out.

CHAPTER
·⋅❂ 11 ❂⋅·

In the morning Murphy steeled himself and went
up to Emma's room. He realized that Mae was
right—he was the only one who could talk to Emma.
The problem was that he didn't know what to say.

He knocked shyly on her door. "Emma?"

"Yes," said Emma. She was standing over her carpetbag, which was at the foot of her bed.

"Emma, I want to talk to you," said Murphy. He
held Emma's sonnet in his hand. His hand shook a
little, and it embarrassed him. He could take on wild
horses and grizzly bears, but apparently a fourteen-
year-old girl with a crush on him was enough to turn
him into pudding.

Emma took the paper from Murphy's hand. "This
is my sonnet," she said innocently. "Where did you
get it?"

"In the loft . . . it was on my cot," said Murphy,
feeling confused.

"On your cot?" exclaimed Emma. "Why, I've been
looking all over for it. I was going to give it to Miss
Woodward. You see, it's not very good, and I thought
she could help me with it."

Murphy stared at the girl with relief. "You mean you didn't leave it there for me?"

Emma turned her back to Murphy. "Why would I do that?" she asked evenly.

"I don't know. I . . . no reason . . . I guess."

Murphy wished he could see Emma's face. He didn't know whether she was lying or not. But if she was telling the truth, it was a blessed relief.

"Thank you for finding my poem for me," said Emma so politely and with such poise that Murphy felt like the adolescent.

"Are you coming down to breakfast?" Murphy asked.

"No, I thought I'd go into town with Father Parker. I'd like to see my pa. And I'd like to take some things into town for my pa and Madeline to have . . . some crafts I've made."

"I'm sure they'll be very glad to see you. I'll tell Father Parker you'll be down soon," said Murphy.

Emma watched him leave. She sank down on her cot and her shoulders shook as she cried for a minute. Then she dried her face. She waited until everyone was downstairs eating breakfast and then sneaked across to Murphy's loft.

Meanwhile, Murphy went outside to talk to Father Parker and Moses. Father Parker wore a pouch around his waist. "I'm taking the money with me this time," he said. "If Mr. Williams accepts my bid, I'm going to buy the building outright. It's a little smaller than we want. We'll be a little cramped, but it's better than nothing."

"Well, I'm sure you'll be able to turn it into a church that you'll be proud of," said Murphy.

Just then Emma stepped out into the sunlight, carrying her carpetbag, which looked stuffed to the brim.

"Let me help you with that, Emma," said Murphy.

Emma smiled but clung to the bag. "It's nothing," she said as she lifted it onto the wagon. She sat down beside Father Parker.

Mae came out carrying a brown file case. "Here are the papers for Mr. Rodman," she said. She handed them to Father Parker. "I appreciate your taking them to him."

"Glad to do it," said Father Parker.

When they got into town, Emma hopped off the wagon in front of the hotel. "Thank you for the ride, Father Parker," she said. She glanced at the file on the seat next to him. "Why don't I give the file to Mr. Rodman for you so you can just go meet that man and buy your building?"

Father Parker handed the file down to Emma. "That's very thoughtful of you. Thank you, Emma. I'll pick you up at your pa's when I'm through in an hour or two."

"I'll be there," said Emma, smiling. She picked up her carpetbag and carried it and the file into the hotel.

Father Parker rode to the small building that he hoped to buy. The owner was outside of the building taking down the "For Sale" sign.

"Mr. Williams!" shouted Father Parker. "I've come with my money."

"I'm sorry, Father, but it's just not for sale."

Father Parker took his pouch from around his waist and thrust his money at the man. "I'll give you a hundred dollars for this building. You know that's more than it's worth. Take it."

Mr. Williams crossed his arms and shook his head.

Father Parker strove to keep his temper. "Yesterday this building was for sale . . . now it's not."

Mr. Williams nodded his head. "That's right."

"The last building I tried to buy was burned to the ground. I suppose you're going to tell me that has nothing to do with your not selling."

Mr. Williams took a step closer to the priest. "Look, Father, take it from me. You're just not going to be able to put a church in Jackson."

Father Parker was shocked to hear that his worst fears were coming true. "Why not?" he asked.

Mr. Williams crossed and uncrossed his arms nervously. He didn't relish having to tell Father Parker the truth. "There's a . . . there's an ordinance that states that once a church goes up in the city limits, all saloons and gambling halls have to close down on Sundays."

"So?" asked Father Parker, still not understanding what the ordinance had to do with his buying property for a church.

"So!" exclaimed Williams. "Sunday is Garrett's biggest day of the week. You don't think he's going to let a church get in the way of his making money, do you?"

Father Parker felt a fury growing in his stomach.

He fought to keep it under control. "Garrett's behind all this?" he asked evenly.

Mr. Williams nodded. "Why don't you just go build your church in some other city?" he asked, not unkindly.

Father Parker turned on his heel. The skirts of his robe flew behind him. "I will not be run out of Jackson by the likes of Mr. Garrett." He jumped onto his wagon and hit the reins so hard against the mules' backs that they bolted. He got them under control, but he knew that he didn't have himself under control.

He pulled the mules up in front of Garrett's saloon and gambling hall. The room was full of miners and cowboys drinking at the long bar. Groups of customers sat around the roulette wheel. A piano player was plunking out a Stephen Foster tune. But when Father Parker came in, the piano player stopped. All the noise stopped. Everyone turned to stare at the priest.

"I'm looking for Mr. Garrett," said Father Parker.

A few people tittered. Garrett's bodyguard, Frank, stepped forward. "You're a little out of your element, aren't you, Father?"

"Are you Garrett?" asked Father Parker. He could feel his heart pounding. He wasn't exactly sure what he was going to say or do.

Frank shook his head. Garrett looked up from the cards he was holding in his hand. He gave the priest a sideways glance. "No, I'm Garrett. What do you want?"

"I want to build a church in Jackson."

Garrett's thin lips smiled. "So I heard."

"And I'm not going to be intimidated by your scare tactics."

Garrett stood up. He and the priest were about the same height and weight. But Frank, who was almost as big as Murphy, stepped closer to the priest.

"Is that a fact?" asked Garrett. "You're not gonna be scared."

"I don't interfere with your business all week long," said Father Parker, trying to keep his voice from shaking with anger. "I don't expect you to interfere with God's business on Sundays."

Garrett smiled again, a smile that Father Parker found hateful. Insolently Garrett picked up the edge of Father Parker's habit. "I'll tell you what," said Garrett, turning to the crowd. "I generally don't take orders"—he paused for effect—"from somebody wearing a *dress*!"

The crowd of miners and cowhands laughed heartily at the joke. Father Parker found that he couldn't turn the other cheek. He grabbed for Garrett, but before he could touch him, Frank pinned the priest's arms to his sides.

Frank pushed the priest toward the door. "Don't go looking for trouble, Father," warned Frank as he shoved the priest out the door and into the dusty road. "Mr. Garrett's somebody you don't want to cross."

Father Parker picked his head out of the dust. He felt defeated, and, to add to his shame, he also felt he had no forgiveness in his heart.

CHAPTER
·♦🙢 12 🙠♦·

Emma was uncomfortable in her old house. Madeline and her father felt like strangers to her. She was nervous after her visit to Mr. Rodman at the hotel, and she wished Father Parker would arrive to take her back to Gold Hill, back to John Murphy. Every few seconds she popped up and looked out the window.

Madeline didn't know what to make of the changes in Emma. She seemed like a different girl, less angry, certainly, but no happier.

"Emma," said Madeline, "I'm so glad you came to visit us. I . . . I think about you a lot. How are things at Gold Hill?"

"They're okay, I guess," said Emma, not even bothering to look at Madeline. Emma pulled aside the curtain for about the hundredth time since her visit and looked out the window at the street.

"There's Father Parker," she said. "I have to go!"

Emma's father held his arms out to her. There was so much he wanted to say to her if only he knew where to begin. "Well, uh . . . when do you think you'll come back to see us?" he asked.

Emma barely returned her father's embrace. "I

74

can't say for sure," she said. " 'Bye." She rushed out the door. She was sure that the next time she returned, it would be on the arm of John Murphy, as his bride.

Madeline watched her stepdaughter leave. She knew how much it hurt Ray Walker that Emma wouldn't live at home. Ray couldn't talk about it, but Madeline knew the hurt was there.

Madeline paced around the living room. She almost tripped on an orange and gold carpetbag carelessly thrown behind a chair. "Emma's bag," Madeline exclaimed. "She left it."

Madeline picked up the bag and showed it to her husband. Ray took it. He remembered that bag. It had once belonged to Emma's mother. He turned the bag inside out. "She can't have needed it very much," he said. "It's empty."

Back at Gold Hill, Father Parker sat on a bench in the main hall with his head in his hands. He told Moses and Murphy about his humiliating exchange with Garrett. "I'm just so afraid that once the diocese hears how much trouble I've had, they're going to decide to put the church in another town. We need a church here in Jackson City. Every town needs a church. Besides, it would make the orphanage legal and get you out of those priest's clothes. I know I shouldn't want this parish as much as I do. I should be happy to serve anywhere, but . . ."

Murphy put his big hand on the priest's shoulder. "We'll get that church for you one way or another, Father. I don't know how yet, but we will."

Moses squinted as he looked out the window. He saw a black buggy turning into the road. "Oh, Lord, Rodman's here again. Without warning this time. Murphy, you go up and change, quick! Father Parker and I will try to hold him off."

"I wonder what he wants," muttered Murphy. "You gave him the reports, didn't you, Father Parker?"

"Emma did," answered Father Parker.

"Rodman's coming!" shouted Mae, rushing into the room with the children behind her.

Murphy took the steps two at a time.

Father Parker turned to Emma. "You did give him the file, didn't you?" he asked urgently.

"Yes, honest," said Emma, nodding.

Rodman strode into the schoolroom as if he owned it. Moses stepped in front of him. "Oh, Mr. Rodman, so nice to—"

Rodman shoved Moses aside. He headed for the stairs to the loft.

"Mr. Rodman!" shouted Moses.

Upstairs Murphy opened the trunk. To his horror, his priest's robe wasn't there. He threw his clothes out every which way in a desperate attempt to find it.

Rodman caught his breath on the top stair. "Looking for something?" he asked, holding out the priest's robe to Murphy and smiling the most evil smile Murphy had ever seen.

The color drained from Murphy's face.

Rodman smiled again. "I believe this is yours," he

said and threw the brown habit at Murphy's feet.

Murphy stepped toward Rodman. "Mr. Rodman, I can explain."

Rodman turned his back on Murphy and descended the stairs. He looked at the children, all staring up at him. Mae had her arms around Lizette and Ephraim, as if to protect them.

Rodman put his arm around Emma. She shrank from his touch. "There's no need to explain, Mr. Murphy," said Rodman. "This fine young woman came and told me the truth. At least there is one person here with a sense of morality. She brought me 'Father' Murphy's robe." Rodman savored the irony of the word "Father."

Murphy shot a surprised look at Emma.

Rodman turned to Father Parker. "I wonder what the church authorities are going to say when they receive my letter about this little charade? I wonder what they will think of a real priest who condones another man's masquerading in a priest's robe."

"Please, Mr. Rodman," pleaded Murphy.

"Oh, now you're polite to me," sneered Rodman. "Now that your game is over. I've also telegraphed the territorial office about this. I'm sure they will agree with me that you and Miss Woodward are *not* suitable guardians for these children. I am sure they will agree with me that for the sake of the children's *moral* development, they belong at the Claymore workhouse."

Rodman's eyes swept around the room. "I'm sure, children, that I will teach you the Christian virtue of hard work. As soon as the paperwork is concluded I will return with the wagon and escort you all personally to your new home."

Several of the children gasped in horror. They had seen the Claymore wagon. It was made of steel mesh, like a cage for carrying wild animals. There was no escape once you entered that wagon.

Rodman smiled again at Murphy. Murphy wanted to break Rodman in two with his bare hands, but he knew it wouldn't help the children.

Rodman sensed Murphy's impotent fury. His grin became wider. "I have a confession to make," sneered Rodman. "I always knew I'd be pleased to see the end of the Gold Hill orphanage, but I never knew how pleased."

CHAPTER
·∘⟩ 13 ⟨∘·

The next morning gloom hung over Gold Hill
like a socked-in thunderstorm. Father Parker
prepared to leave. He knew he had to return to the
diocese at once. He was afraid that he might be ex-
pelled from the priesthood for his part in Murphy's
charade. But mostly he was afraid for the children.

Moses walked in on Father Parker just as he was
finishing packing. "Murphy said that as soon as
you're ready, let him know. He'll take you to the
stagecoach in Jackson."

"Thanks," said Father Parker, closing his bag.

Moses hesitated. "Look, if you explain to the
bishop that Murphy had no other choice—"

Father Parker interrupted him. "Impersonating a
priest is a very serious business, Mr. Gage." Moses
flinched at the use of his last name. Father Parker
softened. "I'm sorry, Moses . . . but I knew Murphy's
charade would get us into trouble. I never should
have let it go this far. The bishop will blame me as
well as Murphy."

"But it's kept us out of trouble a long time too,"
protested Moses. "And he did it for a good cause.
Maybe you can get the bishop to see that."

Father Parker sighed. He knew the bishop was not a soft man. The bishop believed in the dignity of the Church. Father Parker tried to change the subject. "What are you going to do about Emma?" he asked.

"Murphy's taking her back to her father," said Moses. "She can't stay here after what she's done."

"I'm sorry things worked out for her the way they did."

"Yeah, we all are," said Moses, but he wasn't planning to waste much of his sympathy on Emma. She could return to her home. The other children had nothing to look forward to but years in the workhouse.

As Father Parker talked to Moses, Mae climbed the stairs to Emma's room. She felt as if her body had been given a succession of blows. Wearily she entered Emma's room. "Emma, Mr. Murphy is waiting for you," said Mae.

Emma faced her defiantly. "I won't be staying with my father very long."

"Well, what you do when you get back to Jackson is your business," said Mae. She was ready to wash her hands of Emma. Mae was sure that Emma didn't realize the enormous consequences of what she had done, but still, Mae felt that the girl's actions were unforgivable.

Emma interrupted her thoughts. "As soon as Mr. Murphy leaves here, I'll be going with him," said Emma smugly.

Mae stared at the girl. "He's not leaving here."

"Oh, yes, he is," said Emma. "Now that they

know he's not a priest, the authorities will make him leave."

"Their knowing has nothing to do with his being here or not," said Mae.

"But he'll have to go away," Emma whined. "They . . . they'll send him away."

Mae grabbed Emma by the shoulders and shook her. "You gave that robe to Mr. Rodman so that Mr. Murphy would have to leave here?"

Emma's hands held tight to the footboard, so tight that her knuckles turned white. "Mr. Murphy likes me!" she spat into Mae's face. "I won't let anybody else take him away from me!"

"Emma!" whispered Mae softly, appalled by what the girl had done and why.

Emma felt as if the gates to a dam had opened. She couldn't stop. "You have plenty of people to love you," she blurted out. "I only have Mr. Murphy."

"Your father loves you," said Mae.

"Oh, no, he doesn't!" cried Emma. "Or he wouldn't have married Madeline!"

"Emma," said Mae in an exasperated voice. "Everyone here has tried to love you. If you would stop fighting us so hard, maybe you'd feel it."

"I don't have to listen to you. You aren't my mother."

Suddenly Mae's patience snapped. "No, I'm not your mother," she said in a low, threatening voice. "But I'm going to do something your mother should have done years ago."

Mae grabbed Emma by the arm. The girl tried to

pull away, but Mae was not just older, she was also much stronger.

"Let go!" screamed Emma.

Mae forced Emma down across her knees. Holding Emma still with one hand, Mae raised her other hand and hit her smartly on the behind. "You want to act like a little brat? I'll treat you like one." Mae punctuated each word with a spank. Then she stopped, out of breath and exhausted. Emma was sobbing in her lap. Mae forced the girl to face her and held her tightly by the shoulders. She knew that Emma needed more than a spanking.

"Listen to me, Emma. Listen to me hard. Mr. Murphy has got it in his heart to love more than one person. Your father does too. So does Madeline, so do I. . . ."

Mae paused. She looked into Emma's eyes. They were wet with tears, but Mae could tell that Emma was listening and trying to understand. "Emma," she whispered, "you have got to give back some love."

"I'm sorry . . . I thought nobody loved me," Emma said and then she couldn't hold back the tears any longer. She fell sobbing into Mae's lap. Mae put her arms around her. Finally Emma raised her head. "Do you think I could stay here a little bit longer?" she whispered. "I don't want to leave everyone here."

Mae sighed. Because of Emma's actions she didn't know how much longer any of them would be able to stay. It would take a miracle to save the children now. Mae forced herself not to think of the worst. "Yes, Emma," she said. "I think it would be all right if you stayed here."

She left Emma in her room and walked downstairs. Murphy and Parker were preparing to leave. Mae watched them a second before they noticed her. They looked as depressed, upset, and sad as she felt. Mae moved into the sunlight. "John, I think . . . if it's all right with you, we should keep Emma here for a while."

"After everything she's done?" Father Parker asked.

"I know," answered Mae. "But she wants another chance, and I'd like to give it to her."

"Okay with me," answered Murphy, his mind not really on Emma.

The ride into town was a silent one. Both Father Parker and Murphy were lost in their own thoughts. When they reached the stagecoach, Father Parker said, "John, I want you to take what's left of the money, and I want you to keep looking for a building for the church."

Murphy shook his head back and forth. "I don't think the bishop would want me to spend the diocese's money, Father."

"I'm authorizing you, John. Maybe if we can get a church started here, I can get the bishop to forget about 'Father' Murphy. At least it'll give me something to talk about other than the deception."

"All right," said Murphy. "I'll do what I can."

The driver hopped onto the top of the stage. "We're ready to leave, folks."

"If you find anything, you wire me right away," said Father Parker.

"I will. Good luck, Father."

CHAPTER
◦∘⊱ 14 ⊰∘◦

After watching the stagecoach leave with Father Parker, Murphy stopped at the general store to pick up some supplies. He was surprised to see a new sign swinging in the wind. GARRETT'S GENERAL STORE. WENDELL GRIFFITH, MANAGER.

Wendell Griffith was standing outside the store. He was a heavy man who liked to joke that he was the best advertisement for the food he sold.

"Hey, Wendell, was the new sign your idea?" Murphy asked him.

Wendell looked embarrassed. "Well, Garrett does own the store."

"The number of signs he's put up in the past few weeks, you'd have to be blind not to know he owns most of the town."

Wendell took a step closer to Murphy and looked around to see if anyone was listening. "Uh, Murphy, I don't suppose I should say this, but did you know that Garrett and his men are asking a lot of questions about you all over town?"

"What kind of questions?" asked Murphy warily.

"Oh, like, if you've ever been in trouble . . . where you came from . . . mostly about the past. I tell you this because I like you and I'd hate to see Garrett make any trouble for you."

Murphy laughed to himself. Garrett couldn't get him in any more trouble than he was in already, thanks to Emma.

"I appreciate it, Wendell . . . but let him ask all the questions he wants."

Later, as Murphy was driving the mules back to Gold Hill, he thought about what Wendell had told him. Garrett owned almost all the buildings in the town, and so far he had been very successful in making sure that no church went up in Jackson City.

When Murphy got back to the school, he told Mae and Moses what he had learned. "If Mr. Garrett wouldn't sell to Father Parker," said Mae, "he certainly is not going to sell to you. He blames you for his brother's death."

"You're right. He wouldn't sell if he knew that was what I was really doing," said Murphy slowly.

"You thinking of tricking him out of it?" asked Moses.

Murphy grinned. Moses had always been able to read his mind. "It had occurred to me."

Moses thought for a minute. "You know, if what Wendell says is true, Garrett is looking awfully hard to find something to pin on you." Moses winked at Murphy. "I discovered a while ago that if a man fools around with a trap long enough, he'll probably get his own fingers caught in it."

"You got something in mind, partner?" Murphy asked.

Moses smiled. "Well, I can't guarantee success . . .

but suppose word got around that we were going to have to close down the school."

"Unfortunately that's not a rumor," sighed Mae. "Without a miracle, we will have to close down."

"I know," said Moses. "But we can use that to sweeten the pot. Murphy, tomorrow night you and I are going to do a little gambling."

The next night Murphy strode into Garrett's saloon with Mine at his side. He weaved back and forth, looking drunk as a skunk as he lurched up to the bar and ordered a whiskey.

The bartender hesitated. "John, you're not much of a drinker," he said.

Murphy slammed his fist down on the bar. "I've still got enough money to pay for whiskey . . . give it to me."

The bartender shrugged and poured out a drink. Several men turned to stare. Garrett came out of his office and leaned against the bar, watching Murphy carefully.

Murphy raised the glass but it fell to the floor before he could take a sip. He seemed too drunk to hold it. He reeled to the roulette table and put a dollar on the zero. He lost.

"Give me another whiskey," he demanded. "Maybe it'll bring me luck. And here's a dollar on the zero again."

The dealer spun the wheel. Murphy knew that the wheel was rigged, and he wasn't surprised when the ball came to rest on the number nine.

"You lose again, mister," said the dealer.

The bar-girl brought him his drink. "Go again, same bet . . . and sweetheart, you stay with me." Murphy clumsily put his arm around the bar-girl's waist.

The dealer spun the wheel again. The ball landed on the zero and then jumped out. "You lose again," said the dealer.

Murphy shook his head as if he couldn't believe his eyes. He took out another dollar and put it on the zero. Just then Moses and Ray Walker came into the saloon. Walker grabbed Murphy's arm. "John, I know you're upset about losing the school, but you're not going to help matters by gambling all your money away."

Moses tried to take Murphy's money off the table, but Murphy clapped his big hand over Moses's. "You leave my money alone!" he shouted. "I'm not gonna lose."

Moses shook his head. "I've never seen him like this before."

Garrett came over to the roulette wheel.

"Go on," said Murphy to the dealer. "Spin the wheel. I'll win this time."

"Please," Walker said to Garrett. "He doesn't know what he's doing. He's upset."

"A bet's a bet, mister," said Garrett. He nodded to the dealer. The ball skittered around the wheel and landed on the twelve. Garrett smiled at Murphy. "And you just lost your bet," he said.

Murphy stood up, lurching. He grabbed Garrett by the lapels. "You're cheatin', I know. You've got this wheel rigged."

Garrett slapped Murphy's hands away. "Go away, Murphy," he sneered. "Go spend your money somewhere else."

Murphy tried to turn and almost fell down. He shouted to the crowd of miners and cowhands, "You know Garrett's cheatin'. You're all bein' taken in here. You know that!"

Moses and Walker grabbed Murphy's arms. "Come on, John, let's go," said Moses.

"No!" shouted Murphy, shaking them off like a dog shakes off fleas. "I'm going to start my own gambling hall!"

"You don't have that kind of money," warned Walker.

"I got money," said Murphy. "And I know where to get more. All I need's a building. I can make enough money to keep the school goin'. I can do it . . . and then none of you will have to fight a rigged wheel, either."

Murphy lurched and stumbled into Garrett. "You own lots of buildings, Garrett . . . won't you sell me one?"

Garrett said nothing. Moses finally got a firm hold on Murphy and shoved him away from Garrett.

"All right, I'm gonna start my own gambling hall, tha's what I'm gonna do. Somebody'll sell me a building."

As they left, Emma's father said sheepishly to Garrett, "Look, he's real upset about losing the school. Don't pay him any mind."

Murphy staggered into the alley with Moses and Walker supporting him. Then the three men looked over their shoulders at the saloon and, seeing no one, straightened and clapped one another on the back.

"Fine job," said Walker to Murphy.

Murphy grinned. "Think he took the bait?"

Moses grinned back at him. "Like a bear takes to honey, I hope!"

CHAPTER
··❧ 15 ❧··

The next morning Garrett sent for Mr. Clemson, the man he had used to outbid Father Parker at the auction for the school. Clemson listened in disbelief to what Garrett wanted. "You want me to sell that abandoned school to John Murphy. That's the same school you had me buy for you! And Murphy is a friend of that Father Parker."

"You don't need to know my reasons," said Garrett coldly.

Clemson shook his head. "It'll be hard to get the hundred and fifty you paid for it."

Garrett leaned forward on his desk. "Listen, Clemson, I want you to get as much as you can, but I want you to sell that building to John Murphy no matter what."

Clemson sighed. He didn't understand at all. "I'll do my best."

Garrett picked up his silver dagger. "Oh, no. You'll do better than that. Don't come back until that building belongs to John Murphy."

Clemson picked up the deed to the building and walked out the door. Frank stared at Garrett. "I don't get it, Boss. You've got everybody in town

90

scared to death to sell to Murphy and that priest and now you're going to give them the building?"

Garrett leaned back and put his feet on his desk. He cleaned his fingernails with the knife. "How much do you suppose John Murphy knows about running a gambling hall?" he asked.

"Not much," admitted Frank.

Garrett nodded and smiled. "Well, suppose the day that John Murphy opens his hall, we cut the price of a drink in half and fix the wheel so that it starts paying customers for a change."

Frank looked as confused as Mr. Clemson had been. "We'd lose a lot of money that way, Boss," he said.

"For a while," said Garrett. "We can afford to. But if Murphy's got nobody showing up, he's going to go under fast. Kind of a shame he won't be able to borrow any money from Garrett's Bank."

A slow smile crossed Frank's face as he realized what Garrett was up to. "You're going to bury him."

Garrett waved his knife in the air. "I'm going to see him sink everything he's got into that gambling hall, and then I'm going to enjoy watching him lose it all . . . little by little."

CHAPTER
·⸱⸲ 16 ⸰⸲·

Emma got up with the first light and sat at her desk. She had a pen in her hand and her notebook was open. She no longer wrote love sonnets. She was working on a short story that Mae Woodward had assigned to all the older children. Emma tried to write, but the words wouldn't come. She stared out the window. Ground fog covered the gardens. Emma shivered.

She heard a noise outside her door. It sounded like the soft mewing of a kitten. Emma looked out into the hallway and saw Lizette slumped in a corner. Ephraim hovered over her.

Emma slipped on her shawl and hurried to them. "Is anything wrong?" she whispered.

Ephraim wiped his hand over his eyes. "Nothing," he replied quickly.

Lizette looked at Emma. "Ephraim thinks we should run away before Rodman comes and takes us. But I'm scared to leave Mr. Murphy and Miss Woodward. They're the only family we've got."

"Come on into my room," whispered Emma. "We can't stay out here in the hall. We'll wake the others." Emma put her arm around Lizette. She led Lizette to her bed and put her blanket around her. Ephraim sat gingerly on the edge of the bed.

"You can't run away," said Emma. "I know. I tried it. But it doesn't do any good."

"But we have to," said Ephraim. "We have no choice. If we stay here, we'll be forced to go to the workhouse."

Emma shook her head. "Please, Lizette, Ephraim, listen to me. Mr. Murphy, Mr. Gage, Miss Woodward, they won't let Rodman take you. I know I'm to blame for all your troubles, but I can't let you run away. Please believe me. Mr. Murphy will come up with something."

Ephraim looked skeptical. Emma couldn't blame him, but Lizette looked as if she wanted to believe Emma's words. "Emma's right," she said softly.

"At least wait," pleaded Emma. "Don't run away now, while there's still a chance. Promise me you won't run away until you give Mr. Murphy a chance."

"Why do you care?" asked Ephraim sullenly.

His words hurt. "I just do," said Emma. "I care what happens to you. Please, promise me you won't run away now. If Rodman really comes to get you, I'll help you get away somehow."

"Please, Ephraim, let's wait," urged Lizette.

"All right," said Ephraim reluctantly. "We'll wait. For now." He rose and left without saying another word. Lizette paused at the door.

"Thanks, Emma," she whispered.

Emma watched them go. She went back to her desk and took up her pen. The words seemed to fly onto the paper.

In class later that week Miss Woodward announced that she had read all their stories. "They were wonderful, children," she said. "Some of them were extraordinary. I want to read you one of the best ones."

Emma blushed as she heard her own words read aloud. It was the story of a girl who selfishly hurt others. The other children listened in rapt silence. When Mae finished, they burst into applause. Emma felt tears spring to her eyes, but they weren't tears of rage or anger. They were tears of gratitude.

As the class left for recess Mae took Emma aside. "Emma, you should be very proud of your story. You have a wonderful imagination."

"Well, thank you," said Emma shyly.

"And this is where you should use it," added Mae. "Instead of fancying all kinds of things about the people around you."

Just then Will ran back in. "Miss Woodward, somebody's coming."

Mae's hand flew to her throat. "Rodman?" she whispered.

"No," said Will. "It's a stranger."

Mae sighed with relief. "Let's see who it is."

Murphy and Moses were outside grooming one of the mules. The stranger went up to them. "Howdy, the name's Clemson."

Moses and Murphy introduced themselves.

"I understand from some folks in town that

you're looking to buy some property to put up a gambling hall," said Mr. Clemson.

Murphy laughed. "Well, I was, but I changed my mind." Murphy glanced at Mae. "I was awful upset the other night, just blowing off some steam, but I managed to talk myself out of it."

"Now, don't be hasty," said Mr. Clemson. "I've got something I think you might be interested in . . . an abandoned school building. Plenty of room inside to put in a gambling hall."

Moses put down the brush he was using to curry the mule. "Sounds like the kind of thing you were looking for, Murphy."

Murphy shook his head. "I'm not so sure, Moses. You know how risky it is going into business these days. What if we lost all our money?"

Mr. Clemson tugged on his shirt collar as if it were a little too tight. "Now, there's ways of working a gambling hall so you're guaranteed not to lose."

"I'm sorry," said Murphy, going back to currying the mule. "We don't do business that way. We're not interested."

"Well, now . . . it's just my opinion," said Clemson, "but I think you're making a mistake."

"How much would you want for it?" asked Moses casually.

"A hundred and fifty's what I paid for it," answered Clemson.

"You see," said Murphy. "Even if we wanted to buy, we don't have anywhere near that kind of money."

"Well, what could you pay?" pleaded Clemson.

"To be honest with you, I gotta go back east . . . I've got some business problems and I just can't afford to hold on to this building."

Murphy scratched his beard and then pulled some money from his pocket. "Well, I'd be almost embarrassed to make you this kind of offer, but even scraping together everything I've got, it's only thirty dollars."

"Thirty dollars!" exclaimed Clemson.

"I'd be willing to throw in another ten," said Moses, reaching into his pocket.

Murphy put his money away and turned back to his mule. "No, forget it, Moses. This man is not about to sell us that valuable property for forty dollars."

"Yes, I will!" said Clemson, stepping forward and almost slipping into a pile of mule dung. "I will sell it to you for forty dollars. You drive a hard bargain, gentlemen."

Moses looked innocently at Murphy. "Well, John, you can't turn him down now."

Mae held her stomach and tried not to laugh.

"All right," said Murphy slowly. "But I just hope I don't regret this. Mister, you got yourself a deal."

Murphy held out his hand. Clemson shook it vigorously as he gave Murphy the deed. "You won't be sorry," said Clemson.

As soon as Clemson had ridden out of sight, Murphy burst into laughter. He put his arm around Mae's waist and swung her into the air.

"It worked! It worked!" cried Moses.

Murphy put Mae down delicately, a little surprised by what he had done. "Let's go into town and wire Father Parker right away," said Murphy.

"Okay, partner," said Moses.

All the way into town Murphy couldn't stop singing with glee. He had outsmarted Garrett. He felt hopeful for the first time in days.

> "Wait for the wagon,
> Wait for the wagon,
> Wait for the wagon
> And we'll all take a ride. . . ."

He boomed out the song in his slightly off-key baritone.

Moses listened patiently, waiting for a break. Finally Murphy had to pause for breath. "Well," said Moses, "you're certainly happy."

"Of course," agreed Murphy. "We pulled a fast one and got a building for the church for a lot less than the bishop expected to pay. That should count in our favor."

Moses shook his head. "Don't try to tell me it's just because of the building. I know that's not the only reason you've been in such a good mood today. You can't fool me. Something's changed between you and Mae. Everybody else has known for months that you were in love with her . . . I wondered when you'd start to figure it out."

Murphy sighed. "Well, we started . . . but . . ." He couldn't find the words to say what he wanted. He turned to Moses. "You don't think that she'd . . . ah . . ."

"She'd ah . . . what?"

"Nothing," said Murphy flatly. "It was a dumb idea, anyhow."

"Why don't you talk to her about it. That's generally what people in love do."

"I couldn't do that," said Murphy quickly. "I can't say those things women like to hear."

"Just tell her you love her," advised Moses. "The rest will follow."

"I don't know," said Murphy. "I just don't know . . ."

"Well, until you figure it out . . . just do me one favor," said Moses. "Don't sing 'Wait for the Wagon.' I've heard it enough today to last me a lifetime."

Murphy laughed, but now he was lost in thought. Things had been so hectic and crazy since that night he had kissed Mae, they hadn't had a chance to talk. Maybe Mae didn't want to talk. She had seemed to return his kiss, but maybe he was wrong. Murphy hated to think that he had forced himself on her. Mae Woodward was a fine, educated woman. John Murphy had never gone beyond fifth grade. Murphy had no desire to sing anymore.

When they got to town, Moses and Murphy separated. Moses went to the general store and Murphy went to the telegraph office to wire Father Parker.

By the time Moses reached the general store, word had already gotten around that John Murphy had bought a building and was going to start a gambling hall.

"I hope you fellas know what you're doing," warned Wendell, the manager of the general store.

98

"Well, I admit we don't know much about running a gambling hall, but we'll get by," said Moses. He and Murphy had decided to wait until the last minute to let anyone know the truth.

Wendell Griffith shook his head. "I think Garrett is up to something. No one would have sold you that old school without his okay."

"Oh, I wouldn't worry about that, Wendell," said Moses. "I think Garrett's just decided to let us be. We're counting on you to be our first customer."

While Moses was loading buckets of white paint onto the wagon, Murphy came running up with a piece of yellow paper in his hand. He looked shaken. "Moses!" he shouted. "We've got to get back to Gold Hill right away. A wire from Bishop Shay was waiting for us at the telegraph office. He's withdrawing all church support from Mae and the orphanage. He's wired the territorial office to tell them that the church has no official ties to Gold Hill."

"Oh my Lord," said Moses. "That means Rodman will have the authority to take the children away."

Murphy nodded. "We'd better get back and warn Mae."

"Did you send a wire to Father Parker?" asked Moses.

"Yes. I told him that we bought the abandoned school very cheaply because Garrett thinks we're starting a gambling hall. I even told him you were getting the paint to turn the school into a beautiful church. I just hope the bishop will change his mind."

"Maybe when the bishop hears that we've gone to all this trouble, he'll see it our way," said Moses. He jumped onto the wagon. "Well, we're bound to get some good news soon. We've already had all the bad news there is."

CHAPTER
·◦) 17 (◦·

When Murphy and Moses arrived back at Gold Hill, Will and Lizette were waiting for them, looking very anxious. Will grabbed the lead mule's reins.

"Boy, will Miss Woodward be glad to see you," said Will. "Mr. Rodman's arrived . . . and he looks awfully happy."

Murphy closed his eyes for a second. Then he jumped off the wagon and ran into the school. The children were there, and Mae was facing Mr. Rodman and Miss Tuttle. Mae's face was red and she looked furious. "You can't do that!" she shouted. "You don't have the authority."

"How many times do I have to tell you?" said Rodman, backing away from Mae as if she were a cobra. "The Church and the Territory have given us the authority. The children must go to Claymore, where they will be safe from deceiving adults."

Mae clenched her fists, wishing she could slap Mr. Rodman. Murphy stepped in. "I'm afraid he's right, Mae. We just got this telegram from Bishop Shay. He's turning Gold Hill over to the Territory."

Rodman nodded with a self-satisfied smile. Murphy wished he could wipe that smile off the man's face, but he was helpless.

Mae had tears in her eyes. "Please," she pleaded. "You must give us some time . . . perhaps we'll be able to find homes for the children." But Mae knew as she spoke that it was hopeless. She had tried for months to find families to adopt the children, but life was hard in the Dakota Territory and few could afford an extra mouth to feed.

"You have two weeks," said Rodman. "The bishop insisted on that. Whichever children are not adopted in two weeks will be turned over to Claymore."

"Two weeks is not a lot of time, Mr. Rodman," said Murphy.

Miss Tuttle gave John Murphy a very smug look. "Then you had better not waste any, had you? Come, Mr. Rodman."

Mae turned her back to the children, but it was easy to see that she was sobbing.

"What are we going to do?" one of the children asked after Rodman and Miss Tuttle had left. "Claymore is worse than a prison. I heard that Rodman beats the children every day."

"Mr. Murphy will do something," said Emma. "I just know he will."

Lizette nodded. "Emma's right. Mr. Murphy won't let us be taken to Claymore."

Murphy stood in the corner. He heard Lizette and felt his heart break. He couldn't comfort Mae and he couldn't save the children.

Late that night Murphy lay in his bed up in the

loft, staring into the oil lamp. Mine's head was in his lap, and he stroked the dog absently. Moses rolled over in his bed. "Are you planning to get any sleep tonight?" he asked.

"I can't sleep, Moses," said Murphy. "I've been sitting here looking at this thing from every angle. I just don't know what to do."

"Well, we'll just keep on doing what we've been doing and hope for a miracle."

Murphy snorted. "Sure, Father Murphy pulls off a miracle . . . a fake priest and a fake miracle. In two weeks the children will be taken away to Claymore. Buying and fixing up the church may not be enough. We haven't heard a word from Father Parker." Suddenly Murphy's voice turned hard. "I don't want those children depending on me. I never should have stayed here."

Moses sat up in bed. "Who are you kidding, John? You've been telling these kids to depend on you every day since we came to Gold Hill, and now you want to tell them you didn't really mean it?"

Murphy's face got a stubborn look on it that Moses knew well. "I never did *say* I'd stay."

Moses looked at Murphy with disgust. "No, you just said you loved them. You said you needed them as much as they needed you." Moses paused. "But you never said, 'I'll stay.' Nobody can accuse you of that."

Murphy lowered his head. Moses suddenly felt exhausted and sorry for what he had said. "Just do what you want to, John," he said softly.

*   *   *

Murphy was up before dawn the next morning. He took a walk away from the school with Mine at his side. He stopped in a field of wildflowers and watched the sun rise over a hill.

"Good morning," said Mae softly as she came up behind him. "I couldn't sleep either." Mae stopped and patted Mine, who wagged his tail contentedly. Mae looked up at Murphy. He had a strange look on his face that she couldn't read. "Would you rather be alone?" she asked.

"No . . . no," said Murphy slowly. He sank down on the grass beside Mae and Mine. They watched the sun reach the top of the ridge.

"Look at those hills over there," said Murphy, pointing to the ridge. "Used to be I'd see hills like that, and right away I had to know what was on the other side of them. I'd go climbing up over and get on the other side, there'd be another hill, and right behind that, another one. I was so busy looking ahead, I never really had time to see what was right in front of me."

"And now?" Mae asked, hoping to hear the words she had prayed for.

"Now I'd just as soon let some other fellow go running over those hills. You know, I was up all night trying to find a way to save the children. I was about ready to run away, I felt so helpless. But somehow, this morning . . . it's a new day . . . and I don't know what I can do, but Mae, I . . . I want to stay with you!" Murphy stammered. "For the children, of course."

Mae's heart sank with those last words. She

104

wanted John to say "I love you." But now she knew that wasn't what was in his heart. She stood up. "The children are all at breakfast," she said. "They're pretty scared."

Murphy stood up with her. He couldn't figure out why the air had suddenly turned cold. "Sure," he muttered. "We'd better go see to them." He followed Mae down the hill.

Moses was dishing out breakfast to the saddest group of children he had ever seen. "I don't know what you're all being so glum about. They ain't kicked us out yet."

"But they will," said Lizette, stirring her porridge listlessly.

Just then Mae and Murphy walked into the dining hall.

"Mr. Murphy?" asked Will anxiously. "They're going to take all of us to Claymore, aren't they?"

"They're gonna try, son," answered Murphy, glancing at Mae. He wished he had a better answer for them.

"We're not going to let them take you," said Mae defiantly.

"What're you going to do?" Lizette asked.

Mae looked at Murphy helplessly. What could they do? Mae had as little idea of how to save the children as Murphy did.

"You could get married and adopt us all," piped up Ephraim.

"Ephraim!" snapped Lizette. She could tell from the shocked look on Mae Woodward's face that Ephraim had said the wrong thing.

"I think it's a great idea. Don't you, Mr. Murphy?" said Ephraim. He looked from Murphy to Mae.

"Why . . . yeah . . . I—I guess," stammered Murphy. This wasn't how he had planned to ask Mae Woodward to marry him, but it had the advantage of saving him from making a fool of himself.

"I'll get your breakfast," said Mae, turning quickly on her heel. Murphy followed her into the kitchen. Mae took the ladle and spooned out some porridge. She wouldn't look at Murphy, so he couldn't tell what she was thinking.

"Mae, what Ephraim was talking about . . . I've been doing a lot of thinking about that myself lately."

"You have?" asked Mae.

Murphy wished she would look up at him. But he decided to plunge on. "Yes . . . and, well, I think it would solve a lot of problems for us. We'd be able to keep the children here . . . and, well, Rodman wouldn't always be sticking his nose in here, either."

"You mean," said Mae in a cold voice, "you'd marry me to save the children from Claymore?"

Murphy's heart sank. He felt sure that Mae didn't love him. It would be a marriage of convenience for her. "Well, yes, if you think that would work."

Mae put down the ladle. It was all she could do not to fling the hot porridge in Murphy's face. The gall of the man to think that he would lower himself to marry her for the sake of the children. "I don't think it would work," said Mae, her voice choked with tears.

She ran out of the kitchen and through the dining

room. The children all stared at her, but she didn't care.

"Mae!" shouted Murphy, following her. "Where're you going?"

"Anywhere, as long as it's away from you!"

Mae shot out into the yard. Murphy ran after her. The children sat for a second and then piled out of the dining room right after Murphy.

Mae ran as fast as she could, but Murphy was faster. He grabbed her by the arm as the children crowded around them. Her hair had come undone. Her face was streaked with tears.

"Mae! Dad-gum it! Where're you going?" Mae struggled to escape from him. "Mae! Now stop right there!" insisted Murphy. "You stop and tell me what I did to set you off like this."

Mae brushed her long blonde hair out of her eyes. She glared at Murphy. "I will not have you make the *sacrifice* of marrying me to save these children from Claymore. We'll find another way of keeping them here."

"Sacrifice! Now, who said anything about a sacrifice?"

Mae looked at the ground. Murphy still had her wrist in his hand. His hand felt warm and secure to her. "Well, you just said that it would solve a lot of problems."

Murphy pulled her closer. "Mae . . . now wait a minute. You know how much trouble I have with words, especially when it comes to you. Dear God . . . what I'm trying to tell you is that I love you and how honored I'd be to have you for my wife."

Murphy could see by the fury in her eyes that she hated the thought of being married to him. "It's all right," he said, releasing her wrist. "I can understand your not wanting to get hooked up to someone like me. It's all right. We'll find another way."

Mae lifted her chin. John Murphy had said that he loved her. "I'd be proud to be your wife," she said softly.

"What!" exclaimed Murphy, unable to believe his ears.

"She said yes!" shouted Ephraim.

"You said yes?" asked Murphy.

Mae smiled. She put her arms around Murphy's neck and nodded.

"She said yes!" repeated Murphy, and he swung her around the schoolyard as the children shouted with joy.

Emma shouted with them. She was happy for the children, especially Lizette and Ephraim. They would all finally be safe. And to her surprise she was happy for Mae and Mr. Murphy too. She could see how much they cared for each other, and for the children too. She realized that she had given up a dream, but she had found real friends.

CHAPTER
·◦᠅18᠅◦·

Mae and Murphy scheduled the wedding for a
week from Sunday, the last day of Rodman's
ultimatum. They told themselves that they had to
get married fast for the sake of the children, but
they both knew they couldn't wait to get the formal-
ities over with and start their new life as husband
and wife.

They drove into town to see the judge about the
adoption. The judge said that he had never been so
pleased to hurry through a set of papers. "It's a fine
thing you're doing."

"Well, how long will it take for these papers to be
filed with the probate court?" asked Mae.

"Not more than a couple of days," said the judge.

"We want to thank you for all your help," said
Murphy.

"My pleasure," answered the judge. "And I'm
honored that you asked me to perform the ceremony in Father Parker's place. I know how much
you were hoping he would be back for the wedding."

John squeezed Mae's hand. He knew that Father
Parker's silence bothered Mae as much as it did him.

They hadn't heard a word from him, either about their buying the building for the church or about their wedding. The only thing they could assume was that the bishop had forbidden Father Parker to have anything to do with them.

Nonetheless, Moses and the children had insisted on continuing the work on the old school, converting the inside into a beautiful, bright, white church with blue trim, the perfect church in which to hold a wedding.

After leaving the judge's office, Mae and Murphy hurried to the church to help with the painting and to tell the children that the adoption papers would be ready on time.

From the outside the old school still looked just like what it was: a run-down building that had been abandoned for years. Moses had even put out a sign, MURPHY'S GAMBLING HALL COMING SOON! He felt that it wouldn't hurt to try to fool Garrett until the last minute.

"Mr. Murphy?" asked Ephraim upon hearing the news about the adoption papers. "Are we going to change our names to Murphy or just keep our own?"

"I hadn't thought about that," said Murphy. "What would you like to do?"

"I don't know. I guess I like Winkler." Ephraim paused. He didn't want to hurt Murphy's feelings, but his name was almost all that he and Lizette had left of their parents.

"Then I guess you should keep it," said Murphy with a smile.

Ephraim was relieved. Happily he went back to his painting.

Moses put down his paintbrush. "As long as you two are back to look after the children, I'm going to run to the general store. I've got to check about something."

"Sure, Moses," answered Mae. "Take your time."

When he got to the general store, Moses asked, "Did my mail order item come in, Wendell?"

Wendell grinned. "It sure did. It's a beauty." He handed over a soft package to Moses.

"This is a secret," whispered Moses. "I'd just as soon Murphy didn't know I ordered this."

"It's our secret," said Wendell. "I can't wait for the wedding myself."

Moses turned to leave. He noticed a necklace hanging from a manikin with a "For Sale" sign on it. It was an old locket with a painted enamel portrait in the center. "Where'd you get this?" Moses asked.

Wendell looked uncomfortable. "I promised to sell it for someone and not tell who it belonged to."

"It's Lizette Winkler's, ain't it?" asked Moses.

Wendell nodded. "She made me promise not to say anything. She came in for some material . . . didn't have any money. I told her she could charge it, but she insisted on paying with the locket."

"It belonged to her mother," said Moses thoughtfully. "It's the only thing Lizette has to remember her. How much material did she buy?"

"Just one dress length."

"I'll pay you for it . . . and I'll take the locket,"

said Moses, reaching in his pocket for the couple of dollars.

Wendell took the money. "Oh, criminy . . . I forgot. A telegram came for you and Murphy this morning."

Moses brightened. "It must be from Father Parker. Maybe he can make it for the wedding."

Wendell handed him the telegram. Moses read it and groaned.

He ran back to the church. "I'm not sure there's anything else that can go wrong for us," he said.

"What's the matter?" asked Murphy.

"We got our reply from the bishop," said Moses. "He's punishing Father Parker for allowing you to masquerade as a priest. Father Parker won't be allowed to come back to Jackson. The bishop wants us to sell this building and return the money to the diocese. He wants nothing to do with us."

"Oh, no!" exclaimed Murphy.

"Does this mean we can't have the wedding here?" asked Lizette.

"I'm afraid that's what it means," said Moses.

Mae flung down her paintbrush. She ran outside and sat down on the steps of the old school.

Murphy joined her out there. "Mae, are you all right?" he asked.

Mae wiped her eyes. "Oh, isn't this silly. It's not as if I'm a child bride. Who would have thought it would mean so much to me to be married in this church? We worked so hard, and I know it doesn't really matter, but I just never thought for a moment that Father Parker wouldn't marry us right here."

Murphy put his arm around Mae's shoulders. "Well, I don't know what we can do to bring back Father Parker. But there's no reason we can't finish the painting and be married right here in this church. We can sell the building any time."

Mae's spirits lifted. "You bet we can!" she exclaimed. She threw her arms around Murphy. "I love you. I love you," she whispered into his ear.

"Oh, Mae," sighed Murphy. "I think we better go back and finish painting."

Inside the church the children were standing around listlessly. "Hey, everybody!" shouted Murphy. "Why all this gloom? Let's go. Let's get this place painted. We're gonna have a wedding anyway!"

"Hooray!" shouted the children, and they gladly went back to work.

Moses took Lizette aside. "Lizette, uh . . . I think you might want to wear this at the wedding," he whispered. He took her locket out of his pocket.

"Mr. Gage . . . how did . . . ?"

Moses put his finger to his lips. He helped Lizette with the locket's clasp.

"Thank you," whispered Lizette, and she threw her arms around Moses's neck.

"Moses!" yelled Murphy, looking up. "Where's your paintbrush? No slackers here! Come on!"

At the day's end the children, Murphy, Mae, and Moses piled into the wagon and headed back to Gold Hill. As they drove past the hotel they happened to pass Mr. Rodman and Miss Tuttle. Murphy gave them a jaunty wave and cracked the reins over the mules' heads.

"Now, what does he have to be so happy about?" asked Rodman, sounding very disgruntled.

"I read here in the paper that he and Miss Woodward are getting married," said Miss Tuttle.

Rodman frowned. "Let me see that." He grabbed the paper out of Miss Tuttle's hands.

" 'The engagement of Miss Mae Woodward to Mr. John Michael Murphy . . .' " Rodman crushed the paper in his hand. "How foolish they are. Their getting married won't keep those children out of Claymore. Legally, they're still orphans."

"I always hoped I might get married in the spring," said Miss Tuttle with a twitter.

"What?" asked Mr. Rodman.

"I was saying," said Miss Tuttle, preening herself, "weddings are so lovely this time of year."

Rodman refused to take the hint. "So are funerals. And I can't wait to go to John Michael Murphy's."

CHAPTER
·◦)§ 19 §(◦·

The day before the wedding, Mae and Murphy decided to take a walk in their favorite meadow behind the school. Mine came with them and ran back and forth through the wildflowers, his yellow coat matching the color of the goldenrod.

Murphy and Mae held hands as they walked. "I can't believe we've got everything done," said Mae. "All we have to do now is . . . show up at the church."

Murphy half listened. He loved the feel of Mae's hand in his. He watched Mine frolicking in the grass.

"What are you thinking?" Mae asked.

Murphy turned toward her. "Ah, I was just thinking that for everybody else, tomorrow's just another day . . . but for us . . ."

Mae felt as if she could read his thoughts. "Are you as scared as I am?"

"Maybe more," admitted Murphy. He squeezed Mae's hand. "Are you as happy as I am?" he asked.

"Maybe more," said Mae with a laugh.

Murphy swept her into his arms. "Mae Woodward, I love you."

"I love you!" shouted Mae, kissing him on the lips.

Murphy kissed her back. "Come on," he said. "Let's go see the kids. I can't wait until tomorrow night."

That evening, as Mae was brushing her hair before going to bed, she heard a gentle knock on her door. She wondered if it was John hoping for one last good-night kiss.

"Miss Woodward?" said a shy voice.

"Lizette? You should be asleep." Mae opened the door. Lizette, Emma, and all the girls, even the youngest, Henrietta, were in the hall in their night-gowns.

"Could we see you for a minute?" asked Lizette. "We have something for you. We've been working on it and we finished it just in time."

Lizette brought out a beautiful white dress with dainty blue flowers embroidered on the bodice. She held it out to Mae. "It's for your wedding."

Mae's eyes filled with tears. "Oh, it's beautiful! Where did you get this beautiful fabric? I wanted a wedding dress, but I told myself it was a foolish expense."

"Lizette got it . . . she—" Henrietta began.

"We just got it," said Lizette quickly. "It's going to need a little fixing, but do you like it?"

"Like it? I love it!"

Lizette turned to Emma. "Emma, do you want to give Miss Woodward your present?"

Emma stepped forward. "I have something for you too. It belonged to my mother. I thought you could carry it with your flowers." She handed Mae a delicate cornflower-blue handkerchief.

Mae took the handkerchief. "Oh, Emma," she whispered, so touched by Emma's love.

"It's something blue!" piped up Henrietta.

"Yes, I see it is!" exclaimed Mae. "Oh, as if I weren't happy enough already. You are all so wonderful."

"Tell us again about the wedding?" pleaded Henrietta.

Mae swept the little girl into her arms and plunked her on the bed. "You want to hear about the wedding? Everyone come over here on my bed." Mae sat cross-legged on the bed. She looked almost as young and radiant as the children around her. "Tomorrow morning," began Mae, as if she were telling a fairy tale, "we're all going to jump out of bed and get all dressed up in our best clothes . . ."

"And we're each to have a flower!" interrupted Henrietta, bouncing up and down on the bed.

Mae reached out and tickled Henrietta's stomach. "Yes, we'll each have a flower, but we won't let Mr. Murphy see me in this dress until the time of the ceremony. We'll surprise him. Then we'll jump into the wagon and ride to the church. . . ."

The next morning Moses had his own surprise for Murphy. Moses unwrapped the mail-order black suit from Sears, Roebuck. The suit came complete with a winged collar and string tie. Murphy had never worn a suit in his life.

"Moses, I can't wear this outfit," complained Murphy. "I'm all trussed up like a turkey."

"You know, you kind of look like one too!" agreed Will. The rest of the boys started to laugh.

"You're supposed to be helpin' me," Moses said to Will. "Murphy, it's your wedding. You have to wear something appropriate."

"All right," said Murphy, holding himself as if he were made of glass. "But only if you promise me I never have to wear this outfit again."

"Only for your funeral," said Moses. "Which is going to be this afternoon if we don't get into town. Mae and the girls are waiting for us." Moses paused. "I just have one last thing. You know the feed store we've been fixing up. Well, it would be a perfect house for two newlyweds. I'll stay in the loft and fix it up perfect for me . . . you and Mae will live in the new house."

"Moses . . . you've done so much for us these past few weeks. I . . . I . . . just . . . "

Moses clapped Murphy on the back. "That's what partners are for," he said. "Now, come on. I've got to get you to the church on time."

Meanwhile, in Garrett's saloon, the customers were going crazy. Drinks were only a quarter apiece. Everyone was winning at roulette. Garrett surveyed the crowded room with pleasure.

"You're going to lose a fortune today, Boss," said Frank as he watched a cowhand win a hundred dollars on one throw.

"It's worth it," said Garrett. "You think any of these men are going to go to Murphy's place? No gambler ever leaves when he's on a winning streak."

Frank couldn't stand to watch the money flow away. "Murphy's supposed to open that old school today, the grand opening of his gambling hall. I think I'll go have a look."

"You do that," answered Garrett.

On the way Frank ran into Mr. Rodman and Miss Tuttle heading for Murphy's Gambling Hall. "I don't understand," said Miss Tuttle, struggling to keep up with Rodman's pace. "Why would they be getting married in a gambling hall?"

"I don't know and I don't care," exclaimed Rodman, "but they're up to something."

At the church the children and Mae were all ready. Each child carried a flower. Even Mine had a ribbon around his neck and a wildflower twined in the ribbon. Mine rested his head near the altar as he and Murphy waited for Mae to come down the aisle to the strains of "Here Comes the Bride." Ray and Madeline Walker and most of the respectable members of the community filled the newly varnished pews.

The judge stepped forward. "Dearly beloved, we are gathered together here in the sight of God, and in the face of this congregation, to join together this man and this woman in holy matrimony . . . which holy estate Christ adorned . . ."

"And God himself . . ." said a voice in the back. Through the doors stepped Father Parker. "And God himself is the author of the marriage bond," he repeated in unison with the judge as he approached the altar.

119

The judge smiled and stepped aside. Father Parker took up the ceremony. Mae and Murphy looked up at him with surprise and joy. "Do you, John Michael Murphy, take Mae Woodward for your lawful wife?" asked Father Parker.

"I do," said Murphy, looking at Mae with all the love he felt in his heart.

"Do you, Mae Woodward, take John Michael Murphy for your lawful husband?" asked Father Parker.

"I do," said Mae. She felt as if she could fly away with happiness.

"By the authority committed to me, I pronounce you united in marriage. Go in peace and may the Lord be with you."

Murphy turned to Mae. She lifted her head and they kissed, tears of happiness in their eyes.

Henrietta nudged Lizette with her bouquet. "It's just the way Miss Woodward said it would be," she whispered.

Emma spotted Madeline in the crowd and went up to her with one of the flowers from her bouquet. "This is for you, Madeline," she whispered as they hugged. "Weddings are beautiful."

Rodman and Miss Tuttle forced their way through the crowd to the altar. Rodman extended his hand to Murphy. "May I be the first to congratulate the happy couple?" he sneered.

"Thank you," answered Murphy politely.

Rodman glanced around at the children surrounding Mae and Murphy. "Too bad this wedding doesn't change the status of the children. They're still wards of the state—"

"Mr. Rodman," interrupted the judge.

Rodman didn't hear him. "The wagon will be by the first thing tomorrow morning to pick the children up and take them to Claymore."

"I'm afraid you can't do that," explained the judge. "Mr. Murphy filed legal guardianship papers with the probate court last week. Now that the ceremony is over, the children belong to Mister . . . and Mrs. Murphy."

Rodman's eyes bulged. "They adopted them!" he shouted.

The children started to giggle. Rodman turned angrily and shoved his way through the crowd. Miss Tuttle followed him out of the church, wiping her eyes.

"Miss Tuttle," demanded Rodman. "Control yourself."

"I can't help it . . . I always cry at weddings," sobbed Miss Tuttle with one backward glance at the happy couple.

Rodman wasn't the only one having a fit. "A CHURCH!" shouted Garrett when Frank told him the news. "A CHURCH!" he repeated so loudly that all the gamblers and drinkers stopped for a moment.

"A church!" he screamed again as he pushed over the roulette table. "OUT! EVERYBODY OUT! THIS PLACE IS CLOSED FOR THE DAY! GET OUT!"

*   *   *

121

Outside the church Murphy stopped Father Parker. "How did you get here?" he asked. "We thought from the bishop's wire that we would never see you again."

Father Parker put his arm around Will. "We have the children to thank," he said. "They wrote quite a letter to the bishop, telling him all that you had done for them."

"I just figured it couldn't have been a wedding without you," said Will.

"Well, you convinced him," said Father Parker. "That and John's wire about already buying the building and fixing it up. I'm going to be allowed to stay in Jackson City and keep the church."

Murphy grinned and clapped the young priest on the back. "You're going to join us at Gold Hill for the celebration, aren't you?" he asked, spotting Mae, Moses, and the rest of the children waiting for him in the wagon.

"I wouldn't miss it for the world!" said Father Parker.

"Well, then, come on!" said Murphy, jumping onto the driver's seat and taking the reins. He put one arm around Mae and started to sing in his loudest and most off-key voice:

"Then come with me, sweet Maisie,
My dear, lovely bride . . .
We'll jump into the wagon
And we'll all take a ride. . . ."

Moses joined in the chorus and so did everyone else:

"Wait for the wagon,
Wait for the wagon,
Wait for the wagon,
And we'll all take a ride!"